ACK ATTACK

Dennie Doran

Copyright © 2011 Dennie Doran
All rights reserved.

ISBN: 1463696078
ISBN-13: 9781463696078
LCCN: 2011911853
CreateSpace, North Charleston, SC

To Suggie

CONTENTS

	Acknowledgments	vii
1	Composted Clues	1
2	The Dirt on Aunt Amy	19
3	The Dirt on the Sisters	35
4	Dirty Dirt	51
5	Something Unnatural	69
6	The Dirty Hat Trick	85
7	The Dirt on David	101
8	Bad Stuff at Tom Nevers	119
9	The Dirt on 'Sconset	137
10	The Dirt at Family Dinner	153
11	Dirty Doings at Trivia Night	169
12	The Down and Dirty Debrief	185
13	Trashed	203
14	A Dirty Lab	219
15	The Picnic	239
16	The Cellar	257
17	The Hospital	273

ACKNOWLEDGMENTS

With appreciation to the Nantucket Historical Association, and thanks to Suzie and Allan.

CHAPTER 1—Composted Clues

Memorial Day weekend. How does the population of a winter-sleepy island soar from eight thousand to thirty thousand in two short days? A jump-start to summer and a promise of what's to come: Main Street was gridlocked, Straight Wharf was logjammed, and tempers were frayed. Despite traffic jams and never-ending Stop-and-Shop lines, battle-weary island teachers, including me, generally enjoy this preview of summer. School would be out faster than you could say, "No more recess duty."

With classes over, it would be time to sort through the year's debris of extra worksheets, unclaimed social studies projects, and the four-inch pile of no-name-at-the-top papers. Clean the classroom, seal the report cards, and the true business of life could commence: summer on Nantucket.

These seductive summer musings were jumping the gun. There was still the dicey challenge of getting through the final weeks of school, stuck in a room with sixteen students who wanted to be there even less than I did.

This time of the year, it is not uncommon to hear such comments as "Are you *serious*?" and "Get over yourself!" coming from the mouths of the middle schoolers I teach. Occasionally, remarks like that might even slip from the teacher's mouth. It depends on whose wits are at an end.

Usually mine. Maggie Marshall, the teacher.
I have been teaching on Nantucket longer than I care to think about. In fact, I am now teaching the children of the children I've taught in the past. Wooly, steel-gray hair, well-wrinkled skin, and a wardrobe left over from the sixties all hint at my age. Overstuffed scrapbooks from every class I have ever taught hint at my passion for teaching. Secretly, (or not so secretly, according to my ex-husband) I am a middle schooler at heart.

I thoroughly enjoy the hurly burly energy of a roomful of young adolescents trying on their new identities. I marvel at the depth of their compassion and am challenged by the tenacity of their curiosity. I laugh at their jokes and enjoy their antics. Their note passing, clandestine texting, and sneaking food out of the staff's lounge make as much sense to me as it does to them, and I am at a loss when it comes to disciplining those who get caught in the act.

Despite the fact that I truly love what I do, at the end of a school year I always feel a bit like Sisyphus, the character in Greek mythology who was condemned for all eternity to roll a rock up a mountain only to have it roll right back down again. As summer approaches, I identify all too well with his struggle. Spit out the gum. Hands to yourself. Wake up. Where's your pencil? Lower the volume. Sit down. Close the door. Where's your homework? *Ad infinitum.*

As the days lengthen and the beaches beckon, my classroom management techniques become less warm and fuzzy and more dependent on eye-rolling and sarcasm. Believed by some to be unprofessional, these tit-for-tat techniques are about all I have left in my behavior management arsenal. My supply of gentle, teacher-speak clichés has been totally depleted. The well is bone dry.

It was a warm, sunny Saturday, and I was driving to the dump. Why bother to think about school? It was much more important to concentrate on the task at hand: doing battle at the Take It or Leave

It, Nantucket's own unique contribution to the equitable redistribution of global wealth.

A thirty-by-fifty shed at the dump, the Take It or Leave It—TIOLI's as some call it with a pretentious tongue-in-cheek—is *the* spot to go on Saturday and Sunday mornings. A steady stream of cars cruise in to unload unimaginable (for many reasons—and not all good ones) treasures from attics, garages, basements, closets, and toy box bottoms onto the already overflowing tables and shelves.

Also referred to as The Mall, the Take It or Leave It has its regular denizens. Dubbed mall rats, these folks are the determined souls who manage to circumvent the Half Hour Only Rule and stay for the entire morning. The non-mall rats—and I count myself among their number—grab a parking place and go through the shack like Sherman through the South. Frequent practice makes the process quite efficient.

Gardening tools and flowerpots are stacked outside with the furniture, rugs, beach toys, and bicycles. As you enter, shoes and housewares are on the right, books on the left. The Mother Lode—the clothing— is heaped in the center, barely visible through the swarm of humanity picking through it.

The clothing "shoppers" speak many languages—English, French, Spanish, and Jamaican—but the body language is universal. "Back off. This is my section of the table."

With elbows akimbo, I entered the frenzy undaunted. Success! A yellow linen shirt, just my size, with no missing buttons and no spots. In and out in under three minutes. Next stop was the compost pile.

A mountain of rich, ashy-smelling black soil, the compost pile offers free dirt to all comers. Some of us arrive in beat-up work trucks. Others come in well-preserved land yacht station wagons with trash cans in the back. A few even come in expensive cars, like the man with the well-polished Lexus and his Martha Stewart designer buckets in muted shades of salmon and sage lined up on the carefully protected backseat.

Hard-core shovelers like myself have the system down pat: back the truck up to the highest point of the pile, drop the tailgate, fill the plastic tubs, and skedaddle. Although the sign at the dump says, Nantucket's Only Green Environmental Park, the olfactory reaction to said park indicates that the "green" designation may have more to do with rotting garbage than with carbon footprinting.

"It's a Chamber of Commerce coup," declares Rory, the too-smart-for-his-own-good eighth grade wisecrack. "We used to call it the dump, then it was the landfill. Now it's an environmental park? A destination for family picnics? Flying kites?"

"Catching plague? Incubating cholera?" adds Ned, Rory's partner in wisecracking.

Less cynical than my wise guy students, I appreciate the fact that Nantucket has made some pretty impressive progress in dealing with the problem of solid waste and sludge disposal. Doing my part to keep America green, I am only too happy to help myself to the composted solution. With overflowing dirt tubs filling the back of my truck, the recycle bags emptied, and a new-to-me linen shirt, I headed home to wash the shirt, spread the compost, and finish my morning chores.

"Home" is a house my parents built in the fifties as a rental-producing summer cottage. It has absolutely no business being a year-round dwelling. Year-round only works if one doesn't use the upstairs at all during the really cold, windy months. Can't really use the two bedrooms on the first floor, either. Or the den. Well, not the pantry either. A couple of rolls of duct tape, a bunch of old wool blankets, two boxes of plastic sheeting, a few nails — drafty spaces, be gone! Sealed off for the winter.

I spend my winters hanging out at a table near the wood stove in the kitchen, or sleeping on the couch by the second wood stove in the living room. My daughter, Shad, states emphatically that such a lifestyle is *not* for her. Each fall she moves into an apartment over Island Pharmacy that better suits her idea of a year-round dwelling.

I have four children — three boys and a girl. Shad, the only girl, is my youngest. My baby. At twenty-eight, she is not exactly a baby by Webster's standards. However, since she is my only daughter, the only one who is not married, and the only one who lives on Nantucket, I have claimed the right to spoil her.

Ordinarily, she appreciates the Babied Child status and enjoys this arrangement as much as I do. Sometimes, however, we revert to that old mother/daughter thing we had going when she was fourteen. I am stupider-than-dirt (her view), and she is a pain in the tuchus (my view). The authenticity of our now grown-up relationship usually pulls us through these occasional blips. Sometimes, we can even laugh about it.

"You learned a lot as you got older," banters Shad. "Why, I remember when you thought *you* had the upper hand in this relationship."

Spoiling Shad, however, does not include getting my house winterized. Even though the price of wood would make an OPEC sheik blush, wood heat is all I've got. And I'm not giving up year-round living in my house. I can crank those stoves up to toasty and almost comfortably ignore the sandy drafts that seep in through the cracks when the nor'easters howl.

Well, I can ignore them with the help of my long johns and my trusty Carhartt quilted overalls. And gloves. And don't forget the hat.

Dressed for bed, I look like Victoria's Other Secret. The one best left untold.

As I made my way down the two-lane sandy track that serves as our communal driveway, I spotted my sister Chloe out polishing her bike. It wasn't the two-wheeled sort of designer bike with the cute

Nantucket wicker basket strapped on the front that is favored by the bike rental companies. No siree, not one of those designer bikes. It was a full-fledged hog. A Harley. After all, what else would one ask from her husband for her sixtieth birthday?

It's royal purple with silver shooting stars and a hot pink low-rider seat. Suits her to a tee. So does the Harley motto, "Born to Ride." Chloe may have a ticket to ride, but unlike the rider in that Beatles song, she "do" care. Deeply. About her family, her friends, and anyone who has the good fortune to fall within the circle of her life.

Older than I, Chloe has been looking after me since our parents died in 1988. "Looking after me" is a euphemistic understatement. "Trying to boss me around" is far more accurate, and thanks to the fact that I am even more stubborn than she is, a total impossibility. Like Eliza Doolittle in *My Fair Lady*, I have perfected the art of listening ever-so nicely before going out to do precisely what I intended to do in the first place.

Beep! Beep! Pause. Beep! Beep!

I beeped and waved as I passed my sister/mother's house and kerblumped my way along the last hundred yards of the ersatz driveway. I skirted the depleted wood pile and backed up to the perennial bed most in need of nutrients.

Nantucket's soil is far from conducive to flower farming. One of the world's few remaining sand plain grassland ecosystems, Nantucket provides abundantly for moors and Northern Harrier hawks. It does not provide so generously for marketable flowers. While daisies, *Rosa rugosa*, and dusty miller thrive without a care, the less hardy perennials required for my summer flower business need heartier sustenance.

At the end of the last ice age about six thousand years ago, the advancing glaciers started losing their *oomph*. As they retreated, they left behind the huge heap of sand that became the island of Nantucket. Ground-up sand, powdery sand, pulverized sand, gritty sand, still-in-chunks sand, and — for a change of pace — sandy clay.

While Nantucket's sandy Grey Lady is an idyllic playground for visitors' holidays, it is not particularly accommodating to those of us scratching in the dirt to eke out a penny or two from pursuits in sustainable agriculture. Hence the need for compost—by the ton. Or by the rickety truckload as the case may be.

As tetchy, long-time Nantucket farmer Joe Parker puts it, "You can't grow shit without shit."

I checked my refrigerator door's Garden Triage posting, which indicated that the bed closest to the edge of the cliff needed the most attention. At the edges of the bed, the curled, nearly petrified corners of last year's newspaper used as the bottom layer of mulch were visible through the anemic looking compost laid down last spring. Careful not to get too close to the edge of the ever-eroding, fragile dune, I began unloading the dirt. One truckload at a time, I have managed to transform a small section of glacially-deposited sand dune into a compost-rich garden.

This section, the last in my efforts to turn stubborn saw grass into a lucrative flower farm, is filled with native wildflowers: butterfly weed, bouncing bet, yarrow, ox-eye daisies, and rose mallow. It's my favorite.

Nantucket's moors offer up these species for free to any and all who venture out. For the discerning eye, the moors will also throw in the endangered pink lady's slipper, broom crowberry, and Nantucket shadbush. However, for the bouquets that I sell on Saturdays at the Farmers' Market and the arrangements I provide to the Artists Association, I need richer soil. The sandy ecosystem of a glacier's outwash plain just isn't enough.

While spreading the mulch, I paused to check on the comings and goings in the harbor. I can, on a clear day, see across Nantucket Sound to Chatham, with nary a house, shed, or tree in the way. Folks today would pay gazillions of dollars for a chunk of real estate like this. My parents paid chump change for the land and built the house for a pittance.

While they were at it, they snagged enough land so that they could leave each of their three daughters a house and an acre or two on the North Shore. This prime acreage offered a magical playground for our youth: a shipwreck on the beach, and Washing Pond for fishing, skinny dipping, and turtle catching. Now that the three of us are grown, we continue to scrabble hard to hang on to our inherited real estate. Preferring to live in our ramshackle houses rather than enshrine them for rent as trophy houses, we work multiple jobs, pinch pennies, and scour the Take It or Leave It.

Chloe, the oldest sister, is a jack of all trades. Blacksmith, riding instructor, and bookkeeper, there isn't much she cannot do. That would include the tiling, roofing, weaving, and plumbing she does on the side.

A lean and sinewy five feet four, and usually attired in something purple, flouncy, and sparkly, Chloe has been mistaken for a teenager upon occasion. With her artfully frosted hair, stylish fashion sense, and sensuous saunter, she still attracts double takes and a random wolf whistle or two. Not bad for a card-carrying AARP member.

Jackie, the youngest sister, manages the critical care unit at the Cottage Hospital. She also manages to care for innumerable feral cats, stray dogs, and an unworthy two-legged critter on occasion. She can sew quilts worth a king's ransom, fundraise huge amounts of money for the animal shelter, hound irresponsible land developers, and drive the Meals On Wheels van like a bat out of hell.

Because of the nature of her work at the hospital, Jackie's naturally blonde hair is usually in a business-like bun. When not at work, her hair tends toward frowzy. The bun becomes a ponytail, and the hospital uniform is replaced by anything sporty and sold by L.L. Bean. As long as it isn't brown.

As the youngest of the three girls, Jackie's dressed-alike outfits were always brown. Chloe's were in some shade of pink; mine were blue. Seeming to run out of interest in color choices by the time she got to the youngest child, Mom always dressed Jackie in brown. Today, Jackie does not own one single item of brown clothing. Not even a shoe.

While enjoying my sisterly musings, I turned over the mulch pile and gazed somewhat absently toward the jetties sheltering the mouth of the harbor. Sailboats, yachts, and the more proletariat stinkpots everywhere, coming and going, clogging the channel and confounding the commercial fishermen.

Ah. Figawi Weekend.

I had forgotten. Memorial Day weekend, also Figawi Weekend on Nantucket. Figawi Weekend is about sailboats and booze. Specifically, it's about races from Hyannis to Nantucket and drinking to excess in the island's bars. Faces that regularly populate the front pages of news magazines and tabloids sail their boats hither and thither with hopes of winning acclaim or at least some notice at this see-and-be-seen event.

Victors or vanquished, they all seem to quell their thirst in the bars at night, much to the delight of my bartending daughter who appreciates the tips that replenish her winter-starved bank account.

Each year when Figawi rolls around, I am reminded of the timeworn joke that gave this weekend its moniker. The punch line has something to do with an Indian tribe defensively saying, "We're the Figawi!" when challenged by a threatening cavalry troop. The troop condescendingly interpreted this statement as "Where the fuck are we?" The TV show *F Troop* picked up the joke, and the demeaning stereotype was cemented into popular culture.

In Nantucket's defense, our sailboat race was dubbed Figawi Weekend long before anyone heard of political correctness. Over the years, the ethnic typecasting has been sugarcoated and the name has stuck, for better or for worse.

Apparently, my mulch spreading tasks had coincided with the arrival of the first boats, and I paused briefly to appreciate the Norman Rockwell-ness of the moment. Short on time and low on energy, I reluctantly put the dirt-encrusted gloves back on and finished up the last of my chores.

Drudging along, I vowed that someday I was going to buy a new shovel — one that actually has a honed, V-shaped blade rather than an undulating, rust-pitted blade that wouldn't cut tofu. Since today was clearly not that day, I had no choice but to use twice the effort to accomplish half the result.

Efficiency has never been my strong point, and taking a straight line as the shortest distance between two points has never been my first choice. I favor something a little more meandering, something less direct. It's the process I enjoy, not the goal.

Slogging away while keeping at least some of my attention on my work, I began to notice far too many shreds of white paper scattered throughout the mulch. While it is not unusual to find unwelcomed debris in the dump's compost, this white matter was decidedly different from the usual glass, plastic, and metal that sometimes gets past the eagled-eyed Dump Ladies and into the compostable trash.

Intrigued, or perhaps just bored (how riveting can it be to shovel dirt?), I started sorting out the tattered pieces.

Hmmm...shredded paper from industrial strength containers? Containers for phosphorous. A great deal of phosphorous.

Cripes. I could only hope that the dumpers were more careful about using the phosphorous than they had been about disposing the containers. Through the years, high concentrations of phosphorous fertilizers have been washing into the harbor and wrecking havoc on our scallop beds and fragile eel grass.

In the middle of my worries, my cell phone rang. The ring was distinctive. The Rolling Stones' "Nineteenth Nervous Breakdown."

That ring could only mean one thing. My aunt was calling.

Damn.

CHAPTER 2 — The Dirt on Aunt Amy

Crusty and determined at ninety, my aunt Amy-Ann Compton Delano wanted me to get her organized for a four-day stay in her apartment at Sherburne Commons, Nantucket's senior living community. If Amy Delano wanted to spend four days at Sherburne Commons, it would happen. Likewise, if Amy Delano wanted to spend four days on the moon, it would happen.

A force to be reckoned with, Aunt Amy has been having it her way most of her life. As family matriarch, island institution, and the prime mover and shaker behind the establishment of most of the island's social services, Amy-Ann Delano has more island plaques dedicated to her than Madaket Millie's dogs had fleas.

Madaket Millie, an iconic island character, served as a warrant officer in the Coast Guard way before women were actually allowed to do such things. She was also reputed to have killed a three hundred pound shark in Hither Creek—another thing not usually done by women. Sharks notwithstanding, Millie was renowned for her dedication to animals. It goes without saying: her dogs probably didn't really have fleas.

Madaket Millie's dogs may have been flea-less, but Aunt Amy was far from plaque-less. The Cottage Hospital, the library (our Athenaeum), the Boys & Girls Club, and most recently, Sherburne Commons, all "owe her big-time," as my students are wont to say. The plaques in these community-important institutions pay the usual appreciative tribute to her: "vigorous determination," "discerning foresight," "tireless efforts." Not a one of them cites acerbic verbal cattle prodding, which is the true secret of her success.

Many people find that it is not easy to breach Amy Delano's defenses. However, a peek behind her off-putting, ninety-eight pound façade reveals a solid core of kind-hearted generosity and holistic tolerance. Quite the opposite of a steel hammer inside a velvet glove, Aunt Amy is a butter-soft heart behind a hard-as-nails veneer.

"Butter-soft in the gourd these days; fruit cake material," commented Rose Turner, her life-long friend and nearby neighbor. Although Rose was probably referring more specifically to my aunt's recent penchant for bizarre clothing combinations, it is also hard to miss the increasingly impulsive, screwball non sequiturs.

While Aunt Amy's barbed comments are beginning to seem more zany than astute, there is still no storyteller quite like her. She can spin a yarn (or, in whaling parlance, a gam) with more life-like details and appreciation for the absurd than the ole sea dogs who were passed between those nineteenth-century whaling ships in their gamming chairs. The ship captains recounted their exploits in the South Pacific, bragged about the number of oil barrels in their holds, and traded news from home. Aunt Amy tells uproarious tales of family foibles, recounts little-known anecdotes about Nantucket's history, and trades news about island miscreants — both past and present.

"Nineteenth Nervous Breakdown." Still ringing. Gritting my teeth, I answered the phone.

"Plants. You've gotta water my plants."

Not, "Hello, Maggie. How are you? This is your aunt calling."

No. I got, "Plants."

Apparently, when Aunt Amy left Hulbert Avenue this morning, she had forgotten to water her plants. As pronounced, I was to water them. And get the forgotten knitting bag, and her red leather suitcase. Oh, and would I mind checking the bird feeder?

Like some fortunate Nantucketers, Aunt Amy owns a sturdy, well-insulated winter house in town as well as a comfy, Victorian-era house on the beach for summer. Why she would want to leave her summer home and her ever-present children, grandchildren, and great-grandchildren was beyond me. The quarter board on the front of her house reads Pair o' Dice. A play on words reflecting the funding for the property's initial down payment, Pair o' Dice easily meets the criteria for the inferred paradise. Not something one vacates on a whim.

Ordinarily, Aunt Amy chooses to spend most of each summer day on her porch monitoring the activities in *her* harbor while whizzing through the *New York Times* crossword puzzle—in ink. While filling in all those little squares and keeping an eye on the harbor, she screens the police, fire, and Coast Guard bands on her very own BC355C Scanner. Aunt Amy often knows about island calamities well before those involved even realize they are in a jam.

She also has very definite ideas about how these situations should be handled.

Luckily for the island's first responders, an ancient black porch phone with a salt-rusted dialing wheel is her only means of contacting them. By the time Aunt Amy finds the correctly numbered dial hole, pushes the resistant wheel around the dial, and begins barking her orders, the police band is usually squawking to inform listeners that the first responders have the situation well in hand. This news is summarily ignored.

My aunt had purchased her apartment at Sherburne two years ago as a winter residence for "one of these days." In Aunt Amy's mind, this yet-to-come residency would happen in the very distant future. "When I'm old, decrepit, and dodgy in the head." Her family felt that she had reached the dodgy benchmark quite a while ago. The future was now. No one, however, was foolish enough to actually tell her that.

After starting our phone call with "Plants," Aunt Amy finished it with, "Key. You'll need the key." Click.

Sigh.

No sense calling her back. She never answers. I'd have to drive to Sherburne, conduct the usual bothersome where's Aunt Amy search, get her key, and then drive over to Hulbert Avenue to fetch and water.

One last glance at the sailboats, a mental note to finish mulching the lupines, and another self-indulgent sigh. I'd get back to the gardens and the phosphorous puzzle later. Tools stowed, hands more or less scrubbed, I was back in the truck and on the road. With no other traffic on the backroad shortcuts, I blasted the radio and got to Sherburne well before Patsy Kline had finished falling to pieces. A check at the front desk confirmed the expected. "Nope. Haven't seen your aunt."

She wasn't in her apartment or the dining room. No one had seen her at Bingo, she hadn't gone to the day room, and she wasn't at the mahjong tables. "Saw her at breakfast, in her new exercise suit," said Jean Rockwell, the whey-faced volunteer parked in front of the TV in the staff lounge. "Said she was going to try out her new hips."

Sure enough, there she was in Sherburne's second-floor fitness room, power limping on the treadmill with ear buds plugged into the TV monitor and wearing her brand new exercise suit.

Lavender spandex?

The geriatric Olympian was absorbed in the travel channel, watching some ill-advised journalist consume a many-legged creature smothered in a bilious green sauce. Chuckling softly to herself and muttering something that sounded suspiciously like "Son of a bitch."

As she caught sight of me, Aunt Amy, forgetting that *she* was the one wearing the ear plugs, bellowed, "Scorpions. Grilled scorpions with jalapeño sauce." And even louder, "Arizona, the Grand Canyon, grilled scorpions. We're going."

"Can't wait."

I managed a Charades-like communication to indicate that I needed her house key. Directed to the faded Brant Point Tennis bag in which I might find it, I rooted through layers of crumpled tissues, empty tubes of blood-red lipstick, a dog-eared copy of *Lady Chatterley's Lover*, a red plastic fire truck, and — dear God — her gun. I found the key at the very bottom, with sandy gum wrappers, golf tees, and a Dreamland ticket stub from a 1959 showing of *The Sound of Music*.

"Be back in about a half hour. Where will you be?"

"Home, of course," she lied. She's never home.

Knowing I would have to do the high and low search thing yet again, I left Aunt Amy to enjoy her culinary abominations and headed off to pick up her suitcase and knitting bag, water the plants, and check the bird feeder. With luck I would be back home within the hour.

There are no backroad shortcuts between Sherburne Commons and Hulbert Avenue, and getting from here to there was a main-roads-only nightmare. It was Memorial Day weekend; time for the incoming deluge of Land Rovers with acronymic license plates—LOVNAN, ACKNOW, NANTK—most of them idling between me and my destination.

The Summer Specials, seasonal police officers with an average age of eighteen and a uniform to embarrass a park ranger, were out in force, attempting to look all scowly and authoritative. Not easy to pull off from the back of a bicycle. The Boy Scout outfit doesn't help much either.

The usual six-minute drive to Aunt Amy's house took a tiresome twenty-eight, and I was none too delighted to find that I couldn't park anywhere near the place. Cars parked catawampus on the grass and snubbed into the privet filled all four driveway spaces and blocked the front gate. Oddly, nearly all were identical black SUVs.

I figured Senator Marques must be here for the holiday weekend and the Figawi races, and the Secret Service was there to keep him safe. Of course,

26

Senator Marques has been coming and going from Nantucket for years without such elaborate security precautions. Even as a presidential candidate, he wasn't guarded by that many men in dark suits talking surreptitiously into their collars. Something else must be afoot.

Choosing between completing Aunt Amy's errand and figuring out what was going on at her neighbor's, I opted to complete the errand. It was sorta like choosing between having stewed prunes or French toast for breakfast when all that's available in the larder is stewed prunes. Not really a choice at all.

Walking the inconvenient distance from my Walsh Street parking place to Aunt Amy's front gate proved to be a waste of time. A surly black-suited chap in dark glasses made it quite clear that I was not going to be allowed in the house. Or even through the gate.

Obviously, *he* had never met Amy-Ann Compton Delano. My pathetically dramatic description of the verbal thrashing in my immediate future should I return to Sherburne empty-handed fell on deaf ears. Well, one deaf ear. The other was clogged with some apparatus attached to his jacket pocket by a snake-like spiral cord. I hoped it was as uncomfortable as it looked.

Gruffly ignoring my repeated and rather whiney (I admit) entreaties, he pointed with a high-and-mighty motion and sent me on my way — with his growly, look-alike underling.

"Are you following me? *Escorting* me? I mean really — you're going *with* me?"

No response.

As I reached my truck, I fired over my shoulder, "*See*? I was perfectly capable of getting to my truck all by myself."

Still no response.

"Hey! Did you just write down my license plate number?"

A response, but not for me. A whisper into his shirt collar.

Wondering if Aunt Amy knew that her house was noosed up tighter than a banker's bowtie, I drove dispiritedly back to Sherburne. No suitcase, no knitting bag, and thirsty plants. There would be music to face.

Grateful that there were fewer traffic tangles to slow me down and none of those calamities Aunt Amy loves to micromanage blocking the roadways,

28

I urged my protesting truck up the steep, cobbled hill from Beach Street to Cliff Road.

As I reached the top of the hill, I could almost hear my aunt's voice, "Money. More money than God," announces my aunt *every* time we pass the dignified, old-money houses on the Cliff — totally oblivious to the fact that she was making this pronouncement from her very own glass house.

Although we Marshalls — the poor relations — grew up in a house of the nothing-special variety, my sister Jackie went to boarding school with a girl who summered in one of the distinguished ones. Vaguely keeping in touch with Melissa through the years, Jackie was invited there to tea (yes, tea!) a few years ago.

Arriving at the door with her latest two-legged rescue operation — a tattooed, long-haired, practicing hippie with a creative array of facial piercings — Jackie was met by Melissa's butler. Greeted with a chilly, arrogant sort of huff, she began to suspect that she and Melissa might have taken divergent life paths. One look at her Peter Pan collar shirt, diamond circle pin, and powder blue sweater set confirmed any doubts Jackie might have had.

Needless to say, my sister was not invited back. Nor was her tattooed friend.

Navigating my way back to Sherburne without incident, I began making the usual where's Aunt Amy rounds. After fruitlessly scouring her usual haunts, I found her with her glass of white Zinfandel seated at the bridge table in the day room airily making her bid.

"Three and a half hearts."

"Amy-Ann, you know perfectly well there's simply no such thing as three and a half anything. It's three or four," drawled the venerable Mary Dongee, touching an embroidered hankie to her frustrated brow.

"A wee bit tight, aren't you, my dear?" This from Myrtle MacDonald, well into her usual martini.

"*Raaawther*," snapped the less tolerant, teetotaling Kitty Shanks. "And, as usual, making a mockery of the rules. Disgraceful."

While the other three bridge players quibbled about Hoyle and berated those who indulged in mid-day tippling, I whispered my failed-errand news.

My wincing, "Sorry, Aunt Amy," was met with silence.

No commentary about mealy-mouthed nieces and self-important Secret Service employees?

Nothing. Just a vague, thoughtful nod.

Probably hadn't heard me.

"I *said*, I couldn't get your suitcase or your kni — "

"Heard you. Heard you the first time. No need to natter on." A dismissive wave.

No, "How dare they?" or "Surely they don't know with whom they are dealing!" I wasn't ordered straight back or even chided for failing to carry out her wishes. Nothing but an absent-minded pat on the arm and a muttered, "Guess they weren't kidding."

Not waiting around to find out who *they* might be and what they weren't kidding about, I scuttled back to my truck, anxious to get home and finish up the morning's errands. It was a holiday weekend, the weather was postcard perfect, the weekend clock was ticking, and a celebration was called for. Grab a few cookout supplies at Stop and Shop, zip home, finish up my gardening, then fire up the grill.

Nope. Judging by all the traffic, it would be a forty-five-minute wait to get into the parking lot, and another twenty or so to find a place to park.

During the tourist season, the only way to get in and out of the Stop and Shop to grab a quick something is to get there before seven o'clock in the morning. The trade-off is that the help's a little sleepier, possibly a bit surlier. Sluggish service for aisle space; churlish attitudes for a lower blood pressure.

Unwilling to strain my assorted blood pressure meds, I opted to make do with the cookout supplies on hand at the house. Surely peanut butter and honey is as acceptable at a cookout as it is in a lunch box. I would dig out the plastic ware, sit on the ground, and have myself a high ole time.

The morning's phosphorous worries sent me and my picnic to the computer rather than the backyard. Sprinkling my keyboard with Portuguese bread crumbs and dribbles of orange blossom honey, I followed links to such things as glyphosate, phosphorous sesquisulfide, and tributylphosphate. Despite the daunting pronunciations and the scientific jargon, I managed to glean information about everything from fertilizers and pesticides to incendiary bombs, cap gun ammunition, and detergents.

I wasn't particularly thrilled with what I learned about having high concentrations of phosphorous in the soil and the groundwater, so I considered giving someone in Officialdom a call. Surely, that someone would do something with the information about illegal dumping at the landfill. Investigate? Alert higher authorities? Contact the EPA? Write a memo?

Something?

Probably not.

Like Pooh, the Bear with Little Brain, I am usually content with a wait-and-see attitude. This time was no exception. Approaching life with my own version of a Taoist outlook, I am content to allow the world to unfold without feeling the need to bend, shape, or control it. As directed by Lao-Tzu, I try to empty my mind of judgments, detach from desires, and let all things take their course.

With just a touch of smugness, I think of myself as tolerantly detached, centered, grounded, serene.

My family thinks of me as a bit daft. A ditz.

CHAPTER 3 — The Dirt on the Sisters

Ditzy and daft or serenely centered, I was shelving my worries. Time to mark the holiday with something more celebratory than a computer, a crumbly sandwich, and a plastic plate. Perhaps Jackie was home and in the mood for a bit of mischief. Maybe she had something cookout-like to eat. Perhaps an un-cookout-like martini or two.

Walking up the narrow path from my house to hers, I couldn't help but wonder for the umpteenth time what in the world she was going to do with the flame-red travel trailer perched on cinder blocks in her side yard. While it wouldn't be unusual to see a yard-ditched trailer rusting away in any number of places, none of those places would be on Nantucket.

Nantucket is not the sort of place for mobile homes, discarded or otherwise. The live-in kind of trailers, occupied or junked, are expressly forbidden by a whole array of red tape producers: the Historical District Commission, the Department of Human Resources, the Health Department, the Chamber of Commerce, and nearly all neighborhood associations. Most compelling of all is local custom — it just isn't done.

"It may not be done," Jackie points out somewhat ironically, "but it just got done. None of the neighbors complained, either."

Chloe and I are her only neighbors. Not much chance of any bean-spilling from us.

Also "not done, but done" was taking in a bandy-legged, dope-growing, one-eyed ex-electrician named Boston Honorable for a housemate. Daunted by neither law nor social more, Jackie barrels through life on a course haphazardly charted by her own whimsical compass. Folks may have said the same thing about Chloe and me once or twice.

"From the time you three girls could talk, I knew you'd be giving the world a good talking to," observed Daniel Pollard, the Delano family's ancient handyman. "Folks could tell you what to do, remind you of the rules and all, but it didn't do no good. Just skipper-deed off on your merry way — all three of you. Just like your aunt, Ms. Amy-Ann." The accompanying chuckle was the tip off: skipper-deeing was a compliment.

Perhaps our insouciant, slightly irreverent lifestyles are the product of our Marshall heritage. Maybe the result of our early family environment? Hmmm- nature /nurture? Nurture/nature? Far better minds than mine have attempted to untangle that web. Doubting that I would be the one to do it on this very day, I plunked that thorny issue on the mental back burner next to the phosphorous. Concentration. I needed to concentrate fully on picnicking and mischief-making.

Halfway up the hill, I spotted Boston teetering on one leg, wearing Jackie's lime green Give Peas a Chance tee, baggy yoga pants, and a, vacuous look. His dreadlocks were wrapped in a glow-in-the-dark orange scarf, and his hands were steepled in front of his chest. To the terminally near-sighted, it might be a Standing Tree pose. To the terminally skeptical, it was a joke.

Bona fide or faux, Boston wasn't likely to be very far away from Jackie. Enmeshed in that Velcro-love stage usually associated with adolescent puppy love, Jackie spends every non-working hour with Boston. Since Boston has no working hours to worry about, he can generously offer any part of his twenty-four-hour day to Jackie, the payer-of-all-bills.

Although his real profession is growing dope, Boston accomplishes his weed farming tasks behind Jackie's back and away from the eyes of the law. Consequently, it appears to starry-eyed Jackie and to most of the outside world that he is merely an unemployed electrical contractor. However, my high school snitches are only too happy to set me straight. According to them, Boston's dope is the best on the street.

Our family's appraisal of the situation is not quite so generous. Descriptors such as slacker, money-grubbing leech, and mooching s.o.b fall with regularity into most conversations about Boston. Jackie's spirited defense of him is a repetitive, tedious chronicle of injustice, a mind-numbing inventory of minority oppression. An indisputable bore, even to the most generous of us.

Poor Boston has been (according to my sister) victimized, marginalized, and demeaned by myriad stereotypes left over from centuries of ethnic subjugation. His first name, Boston, pays tribute to his black heritage and a real or imagined connection to Absalom Boston, Nantucket's first African-American whaling captain to lead an entirely black crew. His last name, Honorable, pays similar tribute to his alleged Wampanoag lineage. Dorcas Honorable, who died in 1855 in the town's poorhouse, was Nantucket's last living, full-blooded Wampanoag. An artfully constructed heartstring-tugger, his name embraces both Native and black American lineage.

Whether Jackie's beau could chart more than an imagined connection to either of these noble lines is in doubt. Rumor has it that merely a year ago Boston Honorable had lived in Mississippi under the name of Tyrone Jackson, and was the father of at least three illegitimate children. Of course, that might just be rumor. And I might be the bullet-dodging Anastasia.

Preferring to make merry rather than spar with my sister, I ignored Boston/Tyrone, refrained from yet another comment about his values, his less-than-legal lifestyle, and his sticky-fingered stranglehold on her bank account. Instead, I suggested we make another pitcher of whatever she had just polished off, resurrect last summer's battered, webbed chairs from under the deck, and head down to the beach.

Always agreeable to anything resembling a party, Jackie refilled the pitcher, grabbed the chairs, and followed me and my snacks down to the beach. Never choosing to spend more time with me than necessary, Boston headed off in the opposite direction, his keys and a beer in hand. Jackie and I both knew that it was pointless to ask him where he was going. Too old to use the tried and true teenybopper response, "To the library," Boston has proven disconcertingly capable of offering adult equivalents such as:

A) To The Hub to get a paper

B) To The Bean to grab a coffee

C) To the sandwich board in town to see if anyone has advertised for an electrician.

Hunh.

None of the above, if you ask me.

The beach, as always, untied my knots, aided perhaps by the pitcher's contents. Seascape or sangria, it wasn't long before Jackie and I unwound and started planning our next AwfulLogical Expedition to Capaum Pond, original site of Sherburne, Nantucket's first European settlement. More scientific sorts might have called it an archaeological expedition, but to us it was an AwfulLogical one. Not an 'awfully logical' one, but one of 'awful logic.' To those of us who are rather fond of the slapdash, searching for arrowheads and broken crockery in a logical, scientific sort of way takes the starch out of the fun.

Our explorations of Wampanoag and early English middens, a fancy word for garbage dumps, is best accomplished without those pesky, systematic search grids that might require plunging into poison ivy or wrestling with prickly multi-flora roses. Our less scientific path, the one of least resistance, has yielded many treasures in the past. With serendipitous archaeology, we've found broken pipe stems, hand-forged hinges, medicine bowls, and wampum beads—all discarded or misplaced by folks who lived in the earliest Native and colonial settlements. A respectable haul for two unrespectable scientists.

As we planned our next artifact hunt, we watched the last of the Figawi boats race toward Brant Point and the already overcrowded town moorings.

"Looks like the *Shenandoah* coming in. Heard Sam Horner is sailing on the *Macie Boy*. Wonder if Ned McClaffy's boat is racing this year?"

"Wow, look at that one—might be *Brizzer's $wamp* or *Pochick's Poor Chick*."

"Busted. You two are so busted. Partying without me." Chloe had arrived. Helping herself to sangria, Chloe raised her glass and offered our usual toast, "Let gravity be the only thing weighing us down."

Jackie and I added the expected follow-up, "Here's to aging, gracefully or disgracefully!"

"And, by the way, Ned McClaffy's boat is definitely not racing this year. Chapter 11. Again," reported Chloe. "Here, I brought some more snacks. Nantucketized, I'm afraid."

"Nantucketized" is our family's name for the damp soggies that seep into everything from chips to woolens, leaving them inedible and/or moldy. Once something has been Nantucketized, it takes on a life of its own. Nantucketized cookies are gloopies, cheese doodles are cheese noodles, and fusty blankets are stankets. Picnic fare in foggy weather might include potato drips along with some cheese and slackers. Chocolate drowndies for dessert.

The Marshalls, like most families, have not only created many words of their own, but also a score of silly traditions — private expressions and shared rituals for our collective memory. Deboccery, one of the favorites, happens each June when most of the children and their overflowing families convene for the annual Family Week. The once-simple family game of bocce has morphed into an event worthy of Cecil B. DeMille.

According to tradition, the opening ceremony, featuring a fire—often out-of-control—and a barrage of hurled, wet objects, is followed by playfully-barbed verbal sparring and throwing down of gauntlets. Then trash-talking speeches, challenges, counter challenges, good-spirited teasing, and scores of "remember the time when so-and-so." A drum roll on the old decoupaged coffee can precedes the formal passing of the tinfoil torch to next year's master of ceremonies, another rowdy speech or two, and then a champagne toast all around as Aunt Amy readies the music for the costume parade.

Each two-person team has a well-costumed theme: Beached Boys, Obama and Mama, The Beetles, Two Stooges, Hippy Hippies, Leather and Lace. Costumes—everything from the elaborate to the outrageous—come from the Take It or Leave It or, for the more extravagant contestants, the Hospital Thrift Shop. The costumes are sometimes appropriate, rarely classy, always clever.

During the blaring of the ceremonial parade song, predictably the theme from *Rocky* or *Chariots of Fire*, teams march down the driveway from my house to Chloe's, stopping by the makeshift judge's stand at the mid-point. There each team presents some semi-choreographed dog-and-pony show for the judge and spectators. From the tailgate of Chloe's pickup truck, Aunt Amy — self-designated emcee and judge — broadcasts a running commentary on the contestants, their outfits, and the quality of their performance through her old blue megaphone. With totally over the top pomp, circumstance, and flourishes, our Mistress of Ceremonies announces the year's winners and awards the Oscar for Best Costume Design: a bedraggled Cabbage Patch Kid doll with mouse-nibbled fingers.

Almost as an aside, we play bocce. The more competitive teams spar playfully and taunt each other unmercifully, usually maintaining the all-in-good-fun spirit of the day. The less competitive simply horse around, vying for awards such as Most Pizzazz, Best Cheerleader, Goofiest Shot, and Best All-Around Style. Never seeming to run out of creative accolades, Aunt Amy honors all participants at the closing ceremony.

"*Aaaannndd* the winners for the Most Colorful Shoes...the Loudest Cheer...Craziest Hats...Ugliest

Hairdo." And the year that Jackie and her partner came dressed as Ebony and Ivory, "The Most Politically Incorrect." Once the silly awards have been doled out, the bocce champions join Aunt Amy on the tailgate for the Annual Affixing.

With bogus solemnity, the winning team is awarded a band aid, an indelible marker, and the trophy: a two-foot high, incurably tarnished, one-handled loving cup. Although heartily booed and hissed, self-congratulatory speeches have become routine. The boastful winners then write their names on their band-aid and, with even more self-generated fanfare, paste it in a bare spot on the trophy. With years of yellowing, curled up bandages affixed helter-skelter to its pitted sides, the trophy has become a tough accent piece to place inconspicuously in the winner's living room for its mandatory one-year display.

Sharing our day-to-day doings is another of our customary rituals. As we watched the last boats make their way toward port, we polished off the lukewarm sangria and shared pieces of the day.

"So when the cops called to see if I could go rescue Jed Lawrence's pot-bellied pig, I thought, what the hell? Why not?" said Jackie. "Never again. Remind me I said that. *Never again*. That lunatic pig lunged straight at my ankles. Nipped right through my paddock boot. The left one this time."

Chloe, make-believe daredevil, had ridden her motorcycle out to Wauwinet, looped back on the Squam Road, and circled through Quidnet. "I was pretty steady in the soft spots. Not much fishtailing this time." Her announced intention to try the dirt roads out by Gibbs Pond next weekend was met with a unanimously hearty, "*Nuh-uh!*"

My turn. As I described the impenetrable security cordon around Aunt Amy's house, we sketched an imagined scene: Aunt Amy nose-to-nose with the grumpy look-alike security guards we immediately dubbed Frick and Frack. There was no doubt in our minds who would end up winning such a standoff.

However, we had plenty of doubts about the phosphorous containers that I had found that morning. We griped and groused about folks who ignore the hazardous materials days and sneak toxic waste into their trash. Warming to one of my favorite soap-box topics, I ranted for a bit about the global consequences of arrogant waste disposal, plastic water bottles, and excess packaging; moved on to condemning our culture of consumption.

46

"We barely have 5 percent of the world's population and consume more than 20 percent of its resources. Furthermore —"

"You're haranguing the choir, Maggie," said Chloe.

"Again," added Jackie.

"Well, aren't you just the pot calling the kettle black?" I nipped, feeling a bit ganged up on. "Want to run those animal abuse statistics by us one more time, Jackie?"

"Snack anyone?" asked Chloe, the advocate of harmony.

As usual, our time together flew by too quickly. The sun was setting and our stomachs were grumbling. We arranged a designated driver (me, damn it), allowed twenty minutes to gussie up, and agreed to meet at Chloe's once we were suitably gussied. For me that meant a shower, relatively clean jeans, and a turtleneck. For Chloe it meant a multi-layered ensemble with flamboyant accessories. For Jackie it meant something sporty in black, a ponytail, and her Everything Bag—a quilted purse of her own design in which you could put a small child or two. Our destination was Cy's, our goal was nachos, and with luck, a brief visit with Shad. My daughter was one of the bartenders on duty that night at Cy's and would be tickled that we had braved the molasses-in-January traffic to see her.

Unfortunately, town was packed—even more crowded than we had expected. Not a parking place to be found.

"Here, use this handicapped sticker. Just put it on the dashboard and you can park right in front of Cy's. Yeah, right there," suggested Jackie, pointing to a premier spot. "It's the sticker Aunt Amy thought she lost at the Angler's Club last year." Hoping she hadn't stolen it, I slapped it on the dash and slipped into the parking place. Seeing two empty handicapped parking places nearby assuaged a smidgen of guilt for the ruse.

Like town, Cy's was mobbed. Wall-to-wall revelry.

"Hey, Ma!" mouthed Shad into the noisy racket. "Jackie, Chloe, here! Three seats here next to the service bar." Following her gestured suggestion, we scrunched in next to the Maraschinos and the lime wedges. "What'll it be, ladies?"

Fighting to be heard over the alcohol-fueled din, we placed our order.

"Got it," said Shad. "Deluxe nachos, two rum punches, and a ginger ale." My thought bubble telegraphed, "And take it easy on the rum."

Despite the demanding clamor of, "Hey, bartender," "When you get a chance, hon," "Yoo-hoo! Another round please," two umbrella-trimmed concoctions and a ginger ale with three synthetic-red Maraschinos on the side arrived in record time. "Nachos on the way. Back in a jiff," Shad tossed over her retreating back.

While Shad worked, we occupied ourselves with our favorite spectator sport — People Poking. It was a family tradition for passing time by making up fictitious lives, personalities, and quirks for people we saw around us. Any stranger is fair game.

We had populated the left side of the bar with Bible thumpers from Tennessee and the right side with Harvard professors flaunting snooty attitudes when a well-fortified Jackie, ignoring the rules of Poking, offered a ribald commentary on the moral rectitude of one of the town's selectmen sitting two stools down. Since the noise level in the bar was formidable, I wasn't sure if I caught all the tidbits. However, I did hear, "neighbor's wife," and "caught in the act" quite clearly, guaranteeing that he would be a shoo-in for re-election next year.

Running out of Poking steam when we got to the three scowly-faced men at the end of the bar, we decided we did not have the energy (or, quite frankly, the nerve) to joke about such glowering visages. I was tiring of the good-natured sniping, and visualizing a Sunday morning that included more compost and more Aunt Amy as well as an afternoon moving Shad back home for the summer.

"Let's go, you two. We're calling it a night."

I paid the tab, grossly over tipped the bartender, shouted an inaudible goodbye, and nudged my sisters out the door. As the designated driver, I was also expected to guide their unsteady feet to the truck. And into their houses. And onto their beds. They have done the same for me on many occasions.

CHAPTER 4 — Dirty Dirt

Grateful that I had called it an early night, I awakened without wanting to put the day on hold until some more convenient time. Last night's begrudged designated driver status paid off. No bleary headache, no swishy stomach. Smugly complacent, I rummaged some clothes off the floor, jump-started the coffee pot, and prodded the computer out of its sleep mode. Teeth brushed, face washed, and coffee mug in hand, I scrolled through my Facebook news; confirmed that the perfect weekend weather would last; and checked my e-mail.

Reading the red-flagged e-mail from Shad reminded me that not only was today the day she would move back home, but it was also the first day of lacrosse practice for the team she coaches. Well, *team* might be a bit ambitious. Twenty-two third grade girls who have never played lacrosse together do not a team make. However, according to Shad, enthusiasm is what it takes to make a team, and her girls were well on their way. Shad reported thirty-six text messages, eight e-mails, and fourteen phone messages just in the last few days: "Hey, Coach, just wanted you to know I am *soooo* excited," "Glad I got on *your* team," "My sister Carla? She says you're great," "I'll be the one with pigtails and orange cleats," all seemed pretty enthusiastic to me.

However, there was more than just enthusiasm on the docket for today's practice. A great deal of humdrum, in fact: distributing the uniforms, collecting insurance forms, adjusting equipment, fitting mouth guards, and redirecting overzealous parents. Humdrum was my bailiwick; enthusiasm was Shad's. She got to run around and play with the kids; I got to putz around and play roadie.

I added lacrosse practice to the to-do list, grabbed coffee number two, and headed to the truck, off to get one more load of compost for the lupines and some mulch for the vegetable beds. As I beep-beeped by Chloe's, she schlepped out from around the back of her house and flagged me down with a trash can lid and a purposeful wave.

"Hey! Will you take this to the dump for me? It's light." The can she dragged behind her was carving

52

trenches in the sand. "Actually, it's heavy as hell," she amended, doubled over and panting. "Give me a hand loading it, and I'll ride out with you."

It took both of us to lever it up onto the tailgate and a push-me-pull-you maneuver to slide it to the back of the truck bed. "What in the world is in this thing?" I asked.

"I cleaned out the chest freezer this morning. Some of the fish in the bottom has been there since the summer we worked on that charter boat. Remember the *Whale of a Tail*? And that gross captain—what was his name?"

How could I forget Fred Taylor? Grime-camouflaged khaki pants, unbuttoned Hawaiian shirts, and a Greek Captain's hat permanently sequined with curled up fish scales. He thought he was just the bee's knees. Used the same ole leery lines on all the female charter boat customers: "Wanna bait my hook, darlin'?" or "I got me a lure you're gonna wanna bite." Yuck. The worst was, "This here rod knows how to hook 'em." Double yuck as he pat-pat-patted his personal hardware.

Trash can loaded, we chit-chatted our way out to the dump, resolutely resisting a quick yard sale detour near Eel Point Road. Although the Mylar balloons decorating the hand-painted sign promised an upscale event, I had vowed to avoid going to yard sales, estate sales, and garage sales since the incident with the hat. The infamous hat. The hand-knit alpaca hat that Chloe simply couldn't resist. The hat with the head lice.

Chloe caught them, I caught them, my students and their families caught them. There was a veritable epidemic of the crawly things. Even Jackie was furious. Lines worthy of Disneyland clogged the Family Care Center at the hospital for days.

A similar line clogged the entrance to the dump, and we sat waiting on the Madaket Road for a good five minutes before getting near the main gates. While the car line snaked its way through the gates and toward the parking lot in front of the recycle bins, I recruited my sister to help with Shad's afternoon move.

"After all, Chloe," I cajoled, "Shad *is* your goddaughter."

"Goddess daughter," she corrected. Her perspective on gender equity in the celestial hierarchy is far left of center, rooted in the ancient worship of Earth Mothers and fertility goddesses. Ishtar. Ma'at. Isis. One of them.

"And you still owe me for the head lice," I added unnecessarily. Chloe, like many Nantucketers, is accustomed to spending at least part of every Memorial Day weekend doing the Nantucket Shuffle. If she's not shuffling with Shad and me, then she's shuffling with someone else.

The Nantucket Shuffle happens twice a year: once in the spring when year-round residents who rent rather than own have to move out of their fancy but cheaply priced winter rentals. Then they shuffle into barely-affordable, summer-priced rentals, probably with a few dozen housemates and a shared kitchen and bathroom arrangement.

The second Shuffle happens in the fall when the well-to-do homeowners return to America and seek responsible renters to double as live-in winter caretakers. The renters move back into the fancy places, once again inexpensively priced for the winter. This Bedouin-like lifestyle makes year-round living possible for many folks who otherwise would not be able to afford to live here. It ensures that there is year-round housing for the island's work force that could not possibly cough up the $650,000 for a fixer-upper starter home. It's a win-win situation. The island gets a stable work force for its tourist industry, and the wealthy homeowners get winter caretakers for their starter palaces. It's only at Shuffle Time that this arrangement seems more like a nuisance than a win-win.

As we shoveled the compost, I cajoled Chloe into recruiting Jackie to help us with Shad's move. Chloe owed me a big favor for the rescue op I had conducted during her most recent motorcycle mishap. This latest mishap involved soft sand and a tipped over motorcycle. Her fully-customized Harley is too heavy for her to wrestle upright under most circumstances. Pinned underneath it, it is impossible. Chloe is teeth-gnashing strong; petite, but wiry and determined. Nonetheless, her resolute muscle power was no match for a motorcycle that outweighs her by 448 pounds. She had to call for help.

"Mggeee, Mgeeee. Hpppppp....hhhhhpppp."

"Chloe? Chloe? Is that you? Chloe?" Hysteria. Mine. "Chloe?"

"Stkkk. Stkkk."

"Where are you?" I shrieked. "Speak up. I can't understand you. Where are you?"

"Pddddd ctsss."

"Wwwh-ere?" I articulated, sure that my slow, distinct enunciation would improve hers.

"P-dd-dd-dd…ct-ssss."

"Are you all right?"

"Ysss."

"Are you hurt?"

"Nnnn."

"Are you near town? Miacomet? Near the beach? Out by Cisco? Polpis? Paddle courts?" Ahhh, the paddle courts.

Got it. Yes and no grilling had translated *pdddd ctsssss* to paddle courts. She was at the paddle courts, sending her mayday through the layer of industrial-weight plastic between her mouth and her phone. Her safety helmet—the black, polycarbonate Darth Vader one—had lived up to advertised expectations. The state of the art, form fitted, face shield locking device had not failed her. It was locked, and there was no way in hell she was getting it undone.

I called in Jackie for reinforcements.

"Again? She's tipped it *again*? Unbelievable." Claiming she was simply not in the mood for another rescue and weren't they getting just a little too tiresome anyway, Jackie avoided stating the obvious. We were both completely undone. One of these times Chloe's whoopsie might turn out to be something we wouldn't be laughing about.

That time, however, was laughable.

"You look absolutely splatted," I told her. "Here, grab my arm. Jackie, lift the wheel. Got her?"

Chloe wormed her bottom half while I tugged her top half, and she was freed in no time. Her limbs were intact; her pride was not.

"Fine, damn it. I'm fine!" she assured us as she wrenched off the helmet and pasted a completely unruffled look on her face.

"Yeah, sure you are. Here, take this tissue. Jeez, Jackie, not you too?" They were both crying. Then I was. Then the out-of-control laughing part.

We followed her home, helped buff the scratches off the front fender, and vowed—Sister Swore not to tell Brett, her husband. If Brett found out that she had tipped her bike over yet again, he would confiscate her keys. Since I was pretty much in favor of key confiscation, my silence was going to cost her dearly.

Chloe should not be riding a motorcycle. Nearsighted and crink-necked, she can't see in front of her and she can't really turn her head to see much on either side. Not a great skill set to have when you're riding a 2006 Dyna Low Rider on Milestone Road at fifty miles an hour. Or anywhere, at any miles an hour, for that matter.

"Well, I'll be switched!" Chloe suddenly blurted, groveling in the compost. "Look at this — the phosphorous containers you were ranting about. They really *are* here."

Slightly miffed that my credibility seemed to have been in question, I joined her on hands and knees. Yep, lots of the stuff. Even more than yesterday. "That's it. I really am going to figure out what to do about this," I cranked.

"Why don't you just ask Aunt Amy? Get *her* all fired up. She hasn't had a cause worth raising a stink about in at least a week. Probably bored to tears." She was right. It was such an obvious solution, I should have thought of it first. *Before* she did.

Vowing to call Aunt Amy as soon as I unloaded the truck, I forgave Chloe for doubting me as well as for scoring a point on the sibling rivalry tote board. I also threw in the promise of her favorite Something Natural sandwich as a thank you for the shoveling, the recruiting, and the moving. Since Chloe is unabashedly addicted to Something Natural BLTs on oatmeal bread with provolone, mayo, avocado, sprouts, mango chutney, and onions, I knew I had secured her services for most of the day.

Jackie would join us because she can't stand to be left out. Although she didn't want to miss any time with Boston and she has absolutely no interest in manual labor, her suspicion that we would talk about her if she were not there with us would be far too compelling. And correct.

"You two are not trusties—you're harpies, airing all my faults *and* all my skeletons when I'm not around."

Us?

Having secured my compost and my labor force, I dropped off Chloe, unloaded my truck, and called Aunt Amy. Forgetting that she was not on duty on her front porch, I called the Hulbert Avenue number. As soon as it rang, I remembered that she wasn't there and imagined the men in black startling at the sound, glaring suspiciously at the clanging antique, and telling their collar mikes, "Quick! Trace that call!"

Not wanting any more close encounters of that unpleasant kind, I hung up, re-dialed, and waited while the stoic receptionist at Sherburne's front desk went in search of Aunt Amy.

Amy Delano does not have a telephone in her apartment. Nope. Having a telephone in her apartment might indicate that she was making herself at home, and she clearly did not want anyone to get that idea, or the idea that she was resigned to stay for any length of time.

Just Visiting read the homemade sign she had tacked to her door. There was not a cup, a glass, a plate, or a fork in her place. Her suitcase was still packed and her toiletries stayed in the Dopp kit. Both were on well-planned display for all to see.

"No time. I'll be out of here in no time at all," she assures any who ask and many who don't.

Nudged by circumstances even *she* couldn't control, Aunt Amy had been forced into residence at Sherburne while her newly installed hips — both of them—healed. Once her hips had mended and she realized the family was going to keep her at Sherburne anyway, she began her well-orchestrated campaign of manipulative resistance. A master of the passive-aggressive, Aunt Amy had stubbornly refused to install a phone, use any of the furniture supplied by her children, or eat any of the food we put in her cupboards.

"Comfort food. Forget the comfort food. I am not going to be comforted." Jackie's world-class meatloaf, in the trash.

"Bread. The staff of life. Sherburne is not life." Chloe's thick-crusted Italian bread, in the trash.

Since I don't really cook, she hasn't had the pleasure of dumping anything of mine.

Stowing Aunt Amy at Sherburne has been an ongoing, epic battle of wills. The campaign to keep her in an assisted living arrangement would fail miserably without the full family's united support. Unfortunately for Aunt Amy, quite a few of her progeny share her feisty spirit; once the battle lines were drawn, she was completely outnumbered by foes nearly as formidable as she was. Many of the tactics on both sides were quite a bit below the belt.

"Flasher. He's a flasher," accused Aunt Amy. "That man next door—Jed Lapinski? Well, this morning I heard a knock on my front door. Peeked through the peep hole, and there he was. Giving *me* a *peek*—at *his* peeper!"

"Nice try, Aunt Amy. Mr. Lapinski's been in Boston all week," I fibbed. Jed Lapinski was in the day room at that very minute watching a cooking show. All's fair in love, war, and matching wits with Amy-Ann Compton Delano.

When her I-live-next-to-a-pervert tactic failed, Aunt Amy upped the ante.

"Maggie, can you come over and talk some sense into your aunt?" A plea from Hazel Baumgarten, Sherburne's Director of Residence Affairs.

Influence my aunt? When hell freezes over.

"She's set up a tent in the corridor and refuses to live in her apartment. Says it's been condemned by the Health Department—something about benzene, formaldehyde, and something else nasty in the carpeting. She's used a roll of yellow police tape to cordon off the door. Spray painted 'CONDEMNED' right across it."

Outmaneuvering a part-time scoundrel requires shrewd cunning and calculated dishonesty. We were up to the task. In a police officer's uniform leftover from last year's Halloween parade, Hazel Baumgarten's 250-pound nephew, Lenny, stormed through the hallway, gruffly ordered Aunt Amy up against the wall, searched her for weapons, and read her a convincing version of her Miranda rights.

"Silent? The right to remain silent?" Aunt Amy screeched. "Why would I want to remain silent? I want the world to know that the very air I am expected to breathe here is laced with acetone, with formaldehyde. Carcinogens, straight to the lungs! I demand a press conference!"

Brandishing cuffs, Lenny promised her a stint in the slammer — without bail. "You're in violation of Article 3, Section 10-95, Ordinance number 2011-17B. Add resisting arrest to the charges and I guarantee you'll be sent to the county lockup in Barnstable."

Without a trace of anything resembling good grace, Aunt Amy dismantled the tent and took down the caution tape. Determined to have the last word, she fired the final salvo, "And don't think I didn't take down your badge number, Officer. Your career has just taken an unwelcomed turn."

64

The officer's badge had no number on it. Twenty-twenty vision would have revealed Tip Top Toys beneath the imitation plastic shield and Officer Sunshine in raised letters under that.

Despite all her failed resistance ploys, each winter Aunt Amy insisted that she was going home as usual to Main Street. The family insisted that she stay at Sherburne, and to ensure that she did, they filled up the Main Street house with year-round tenants. She had nowhere else to go. Her summer house on Hulbert was closed up tight. Her winter house was rented. Checkmate. Aunt Amy was stuck at Sherburne, where we hoped the staff might be able to keep tabs on her. Although none of us envied them that thankless task, we also recognized that a mentally questionable, ninety-year-old woman — no matter how lively or stubborn — should not live alone on a sparsely populated island thirty miles out to sea.

In addition to Aunt Amy's bad hips, she had an unrealistic sense of her physical limitations and was in total denial about her failing vision and hearing, her heart problems, forgetfulness, and increasingly peculiar idiosyncrasies. She also had a sure-fire penchant for getting into trouble. Having her reside at Sherburne during the winter seemed like a no-brainer to the family. Aunt Amy was of a decidedly different opinion.

"A nincompoop! My family treats me like I'm incompetent—a nincompoop," she announced. "Like I've lost my last marble and they don't want me to find it."

We were willing to pay the staff a small fortune, tip them lavishly, and shower them with Christmas bonuses so that they would play nice with Aunt Amy—even when she clearly wasn't going to play nice in return. Allowing her to move to Hulbert for the summer was our ace in the hole, the summer carrot to lessen the sting of the winter stick. Also on our side was the unconfirmed rumor that she, possibly a bit overserved, had actually admitted that the place was "not so bad." Maybe she even secretly accepted the wisdom of our decision. Probably not.

When Sally, Sherburne's accommodating receptionist got back on the phone, she reported that she had finally located Aunt Amy out on the grounds near the pergola, bellowing instructions to the entire staff of gardeners about the proper care of Scotch Broom. Dark yellow Scotch Broom is her favorite island shrub. She has no use for the pale yellow ones, or the designer pinks.

"Tacky. They're downright tacky," rails Aunt Amy. "Best thing for them would be a good dose of Agent Orange. Or transplant 'em all to the Vineyard."

Panting from her irritated stomp to the phone, Aunt Amy barked her hello in a voice that was even more brusque than usual. She softened it slightly when she realized who it was and why I was calling. I briefly outlined my concerns about the phosphorous dumping.

Immediately, she filed through her vast store of knowledge about the island's bureaucratic labyrinths. She then produced, off the top of her head, the name *and* phone number of the perfect official to call. She also insisted that she be the one to do the calling.

"I've known that scoundrel since before he was potty trained. And I know about the kinky thing with horses. And I'm not afraid to tell. He knows it, too. I'll make the call."

Feeling a little sorry for the poor soul I'd just thrown under the bus, I tried half-heartedly to reclaim the responsibility for the call. Aunt Amy was far too delighted that she had a "boobocrat" in her sights and a cause that she, the ole muckraker, could champion. She responded to my tepid, "No, that's all right, I'll make the call," by slamming down the receiver.

Sigh.

Tempted to let the dial tone be her last word, I decided instead to do the more painful right thing. I called her back and invited her to lunch. Feeling a bit like a hapless canary inviting the wily cat, I extended the invitation as graciously as I could. Sensing that a luncheon outing with three of her nieces would be a perfect time to stir the family pot, Aunt Amy readily agreed.

"You're buying, though. Remember, I am just a poor widow."

Aunt Amy said this every single time anyone invited her to go anywhere. Richer than Croesus and perfectly capable of buying not only the lunch but the restaurant itself, Aunt Amy's poor-me routine was given the usual lukewarm *tsk-tsks*. Since I had heard about her purported abject poverty many times, I had already assumed that I would be picking up the tab. Figuring that my bank account could stand the cost of an extra sandwich, I told her that I would pick her up in about an hour. To express her thanks, she hung up on me. Again.

CHAPTER 5 — Something Unnatural

Feeling a mite hungry myself, I was happy to see that Aunt Amy was waiting out front for a change. The hapless gardener pruning the hydrangeas was not sharing my sentiments.

"*Sam*uel. Not that way, Samuel," she corrected. "Cut it there. *There*. Otherwise it won't bloom. And why wasn't this done in the fall?"

Not waiting for the beleaguered Samuel's response, Aunt Amy cast her critical eye to my truck. "Rattletrap. Same ole rattletrap," she remarked as she ran her finger down the truck's well-dusted side. "Tidy...and a tidy interior as well," she added in her irritating matriarch voice as she picked up the Espresso-to-Go cup that landed on her foot when she opened the door.

Aunt Amy describes my truck as an abomination and can't resist at least one remark about either the assortment of gardening tools and schoolbooks littering the backseat and floor, or the discarded take-out food containers sprinkled liberally on top of the debris. She generally manages to include some disparaging reference to the rusty dents on the rear fender as well as the Nantucket Pin Stripes scratched into the side of the truck.

"Nantucket Pinstripes" is a euphemism for the long, tangled scratches found on the sides of many, if not most, island vehicles. Many Nantucket roads are not paved, and some of the paved roads have a way of just petering out, losing their sense of purpose. Their surface paving diminishes into haphazardly spread stone, and then fades into rutted clay, powdery dirt, and soft sand. The carefully planned road takes to ambling and twisting.

Traveling on dirt roads is pretty much inevitable on Nantucket. These roads are not very wide and are narrowed further by encroaching blackberry brambles, scrub oak, and pitch pine — all of which are very scratchy. Because of frequent trips to the moors around Pout Pond, my truck appears to be encased in a fine, etched webbing. Most Nantucketers take pin-striping in stride. Some even consider it a badge of honor — a tribute to their rugged, outdoorsy selves. My aunt is not one of them.

Taking the offensive and short-circuiting her critique, I gave her a lifting tug into the truck and said, "Just step on whatever is on the floor and be grateful that I am picking you up at all. It's not nice to hang up on people." As she settled on the seat, I added, "And remember, you can't drive yourself. If Captain Mayhew catches you behind the wheel again, you're liable to end up in the slammer."

"Jonathan Mayhew. *Huh.* I hope he tries."

Oh my.

There was no point in reminding Aunt Amy that she had lost her driver's license two years ago. She thinks that revoking her license had been "the most egregious miscarriage of justice since the execution of Sacco and Vanzetti." In her view, if she didn't agree with the verdict, then she need not comply. After all, the accident was the result of a mechanical failure and not her fault at all. Could she help it if "some electronic doohickey under the hood" had locked her brakes and unlocked her throttle?

According to the police report, Aunt Amy had mistaken the accelerator for the brake while attempting to park her prized, canary yellow, 1965 Lincoln Continental on Main Street. There was no doohickey involved, electronic or otherwise. Thinking she was jamming on the brakes, she stomped the accelerator, drove straight over the curb, and rammed right through the front window of the Nantucket Pharmacy.

Amazingly, no one was hurt, and David Malenga, the owner, was just inside the front door. Always ready with a witty one-liner, David turned to Aunt Amy and teased, "Come in to pick up your prescription have you, Mrs. Delano?"

A timid, "Ooops" preceded Aunt Amy's, "Police. Dear God, David, don't call the police!"

Too late. Just ten feet away, a Summer Special was busy tucking bright orange parking tickets under windshields and chalking the tires on any cars he couldn't ticket. Overly zealous and playing to the rapidly gathering crowd, the officer proceeded to order Aunt Amy out of the car and up against the side of it.

Standing in the wreckage of his front window and his entire beach toy display, David intervened. "I think we can safely assume that Mrs. Delano will not be fleeing the scene, Officer. In fact, it doesn't appear that she can even get out of the car." Pointing to the crumpled door on the driver's side, David punned, "She seems to be in*car*cerated already."

Aunt Amy was gearing up to treat the Summer Special to the dressing down of his life. Sensing the need for a diversion as well as a solution, David intervened once more. "Mrs. Delano? Do you think you could climb over into the backseat? We might be able to wriggle you out through the rear window."

With all the poise she could muster, Aunt Amy managed an awkward dive over the seat and disappeared into a heap in the back. Popping up from the floorboards in a devil-may-care sort of way, she merrily chirped, "Not bad, *eh*? Let's wriggle."

Of course, David didn't press charges. In fact, he didn't charge Aunt Amy for her prescription—and according to Captain. Mayhew, he even drove her home.

The police were not quite so chivalrous. They insisted that she take the same rigorous driver's test that first-time applicants must pass. Needless to say, Aunt Amy didn't pass. Her license was revoked, and she was sternly warned to obey the spirit as well as the letter of the law. Aunt Amy demanded an appeal, threatened lawsuits, and told Captain Mayhew that he would rue the day he had tangled with her.

"Jackboots. The jackboots think they have had their way with me, but they haven't seen the last of Amy-Ann Compton Delano."

True to her word, they saw her again—behind the wheel—on at least three more occasions. They pulled her over, wagged an admonishing finger under her nose, and drove her home. Possibly getting a bit tired of her cavalier flaunting of the law, Captain Mayhew threatened to lock her up if she were caught again.

"Ghastly. Just ghastly. There's not one square inch of clean space for my feet. Not one," snapped Aunt Amy, struggling in vain to find some uncontaminated foot space in my truck. "Is that ketchup right there? On that bag?" Perching her Keds between the hedge trimmers and the carton of fish emulsion, she resumed cataloging her complaints. "Condemn it. The Health Department would have a field day with the nastiness on this floor."

"So walk. Don't come. Or hush."

She hushed.

As she wrestled with her seat belt, I noticed that she had dressed up for our lunch date. "Nice hat," I complimented a bit sarcastically while nodding at the black-veiled scarlet pillbox perched at a precarious angle just above her eyebrows.

"Quite fond of it myself," she answered. "Wanted something to match the shorts." The hat would have looked great on Greta Garbo, smartly clad in a well-tailored travel suit. Not so much on knobby-kneed Aunt Amy, raggedly clad in a pair of wrinkled, patchwork madras shorts. I kept that to myself.

There's not much that the family manages to keep from Aunt Amy. She may be a bit addled, even occasionally tetchy, but she's got her finger well pressed on the family pulse. She and her husband Charlie, my mom's brother, raised their two daughters, Elizabeth and Alexandra, on Nantucket and were part-time parents to my two sisters and me each summer. Since our parents died, we Marshall girls have been absorbed even more closely into the Delano family orbit. Aunt Amy keeps an uncomfortably close eye on us all. And vice versa.

On the way to Something Natural, Aunt Amy began to fill me in on the family news. "The triplets are teething, Josh arrives on the noon boat tomorrow, and all the beagles need to be wormed." The details followed and I caught up on the most recent Delano doings. Although I am always eager for family updates, a report on the stool consistency of the dogs was not what I had in mind.

Second cousin Carolyn's triplet sons, ordinarily quite sunny and placid, had been transformed into demons from hell with the advent of toddlerhood. Carolyn's mother, Cousin Elizabeth, recommended an old-fashioned swat on the fanny after being bitten by one and kicked by another. Instructing her mother about the psychological nuances of child abuse, Carolyn hinted that Cousin Elizabeth might want to attend next weekend's Parenting for Peace symposium in Amherst before spending any more time with her grandchildren.

"Anarchists. Carolyn's raising a bunch of anarchists," was Aunt Amy's final word on that.

76

It is no secret that Josh, "*Daaahling* Joshua," is Aunt Amy's favorite grandchild. Cousin Alexandra's third child is a sculptor, a mason, and a charmer. The sculpting nurtures his creative soul, the masonry pays the bills, and the charm covers all the other bases. Not content to rest on just his winning personality, Josh is always the first to show up each summer to move Aunt Amy from her winter house to her summer one. He is also the first to show up on Columbus Day weekend to reverse the process. He gets the boats in the water, organizes the work crews to paint whatever needs a coat or two, and teaches the great-grandkids how to sail. He has well earned his favored status.

Josh would be arriving for the summer tomorrow, and this year he was bringing his "strumpet." Although Josh has been dating said strumpet for three years and she has visited Nantucket many times, Aunt Amy still refuses to call her by name. Her name is Grace, and she thinks Aunt Amy is a hoot. The family, with one notable exception, adores Grace.

"Trollop. I guess Alexandra will let Joshua live in sin with that trollop. Right under her very nose," was her final word on that.

The beagles were next on Aunt Amy's agenda, including a not-to-be-overlooked stool consistency report. There are four beagles: Clyde, Bonnie, Butch, and Sundance. Although Cousin Elizabeth had rescued them, Aunt Amy takes the credit for it, as well as summer custody of the hounds. Cousin Elizabeth's dogs are Aunt Amy's pride and joy, and the scourge of Hulbert Avenue. More than once I have been buttonholed by one of her neighbors to hear a laundry list of complaints.

"They dug up my lilies!"

"They got into the trash."

"Howled all night."

"Worms. I don't know where they could have picked up those worms," she muttered. "And I am going to have a talk with that Ernie Whitehead. That busybody has gotten the neighbors to hire a lawyer and take out a restraining order against my dogs," she lamented. "A restraining order — against dogs! Can you imagine?"

"I'm suing," ended that harangue.

We arrived at Something Natural just as Aunt Amy was about to launch into a heated diatribe against the Brant Point Neighborhood Association and canine restraining orders. As usual, the popular sandwich shop's parking lot was jammed with cars, kids, bikes, and dogs, all of them in motion and none of them paying any attention to cars trying to park.

As a Frisbee ricocheted off the windshield, Aunt Amy began directing. "Turn. Turn. Hard right! No, *right*! Are you trying to steer the Titanic? There. Over *there*. Squeeze in there," she instructed as she pointed to a Smart Car-sized space near the bike rack. "Oh, for the love of Pete. Do you want me to park it?"

I was saved from a response that I would probably regret by a motorcycle zipping past on my right side and fishtailing into the undersized parking space, peppering the side of my truck with a shower of stones. Chloe and Jackie had arrived.

"We'll take Aunt Amy. You go park."

Bless you, Chloe.

"Nice hat," I heard Jackie chuckle as I was backing out.

By the time I found a place to park on Cliff Road, they had picked up the sandwiches, added

Nantucket Nectars, Cape Cod chips, a tie-dyed T-shirt for Aunt Amy, and a dozen oatmeal raisin cookies to the tab, which was left for me. After paying, I joined them at the picnic table under the mulberry tree just in time to hear the wrap-up of Aunt Amy's counter strategy for the next Neighbor Association meeting. Something involving a short veterinarian, a long speech, and the unleashing of the four accused hounds at the end. I just hoped that the *Inquirer and Mirror,* our local paper, was not going to be covering the meeting.

Hoping to steer her away from another rant about her neighbors, I asked if she had found anyone who could investigate the phosphorous dumping.

"There was not one single person in the entire Town Building when I went down there! Not one. In fact, the building was locked," she responded indignantly.

Assuming that she had failed to complete her self-appointed mission, Chloe soothingly offered, "Well, it *is* Sunday on a three-day holiday weekend. Perhaps on Tuesday...?"

"Too late. Tuesday might be too late," Aunt Amy said with a dramatic slitting gesture across her throat. "I called Gifford Ray at home, browbeat his skinny-bottomed wife into getting him off the lawn tractor, and gave him a piece of my mind." Prudently, Gifford promised to head down to the Town building immediately and take whatever steps needed to be taken. So much for his three-day weekend.

"I am sure we can get to the bottom of this, Mrs. Delano, he promised me.

"Bottom? I didn't care about anyone's *bottom*. I wanted him to get on top of it. On *top* of it, I told him."

Apparently Gifford suspected that she had not really heard what he said about getting to the bottom of the situation. In an effort to reassure her, Gifford had added something to the effect that he would be on top of the matter before she could shake a stick at it.

Hardly reassured, it sounded as if my aunt had let him have it with both haughty barrels. "Sticks? Sticks? I told that ninny I couldn't care less about *sticks* in the compost. It was *phosphorous*. Phosphorous!" I imagined Aunt Amy's exasperated sigh, melodramatic eye roll, and a slammed down receiver. Many more conversations like that and Gifford would probably end up as addled as she was.

Feeling that she had taken care of the toxic dumping, the dim-witted Gifford Ray, and more than earned her lunch, Aunt Amy began to focus on her own agenda. "Heavy metal. Did you know that the water at Sherburne Commons has enough heavy metal in it to short circuit a microwave?"

There is no response you can make to statements like that; they are ridiculous and complete lies. We have learned the hard way that any response we make other than a discouraging grunt will be interpreted as agreement. Thus encouraged, Aunt Amy will take it to the next level. It's never pretty and it's usually illegal.

Well-practiced in diversionary tactics, we got Aunt Amy to put on her new T-shirt, put all the uneaten cookies in her forty-pound purse, and vamoose.

We were almost to the parking lot when Aunt Amy spotted Ernie Whitehead.

Uh-oh.

Bearing down on her unsuspecting neighbor just as he was about to bite into his roast beef sandwich,

Aunt Amy shouted, "Just who do you think you are, Ernie Whitehead?" she began, "My beagles are —" She never finished her sentence.

Ernie, the ole smoothie, stood and gave her a hundred-watt smile, a wink, and a suave, "Amy-Ann, my dear. How nice to see you. How *are* you?"

Momentarily stopped in her tracks, Aunt Amy lost her train of thought. Never one to lose the advantage, Ernie quickly jumped into the conversational void with a question of his own. "Say, what *is* going on at Senator Marques's house? I've heard the airport has been closed to civilian traffic all morning and at least four U.S. government jets are parked out on the macadam."

"Senator Marques? I haven't the foggiest notion," Aunt Amy replied. "Maggie was turned away yesterday when she tried to find my knitting bag and water my plants."

"Why aren't *you* watering your own plants, Amy?" he archly inquired.

Sensing that a critical eye had been cast on her ability to take care of herself, she added importantly, "I am not *staying* there, Ernie. Uncle Sam is — well, Homeland Security. The Feds; they're staying there for a few days. I am going to get a handwritten letter of thanks from the president. And an invitation to the White House."

Somewhat taken aback that his neighbor was included in such an important loop, Ernie added in his typical one-upmanship fashion, "Well, *I* heard that there's a very high level, hush-hush meeting going on at the senator's house. Heard it from Suzie Del Corazon, so it must be true."

"So there" was unspoken, but definitely implied.

While I was mulling over that information, I realized that an upstaged Aunt Amy was about to regain the spotlight with a full-frontal assault about the restraining order. I grabbed her elbow and steered her toward the parking lot. "Gotta go. I have to help Shad move," I announced.

"Oh, goody! Can I come?" she asked with sanguine confidence.

Damn.

CHAPTER 6 — The Hat Trick

Arm in arm, Aunt Amy and I lurched our way over the sandwich shop's uneven, crushed-shell driveway. It was a struggle to keep her vertical. The rutted potholes, the quahog shells, the pendulum motion of her purse, and the side-to-side chimp-like gait dictated by her new hips seemed to propel her sideways, then forward in erratic fits and starts. "There ought to be a law against driveways like this. And let go of me," she added as she yanked herself free of my grasp.

Her abrupt motion refashioned the overweight purse from an unfashionable accessory to a semi-lethal projectile. Her purse accelerated on its backward arc, torpedoed forward, and whapped me in the hip, knocking me flat.

By some stroke of luck, Aunt Amy stayed upright. "Help? Any more help from you and I'm going to end up in the hospital," she called over her shoulder as she chimp-marched ahead.

Not even bothering to check on my life and limb, she bellowed, "I'll wait for you at the end of the driveway. And hurry up."

I brushed the chalky, white dust off the seat of my pants, picked the quahog shards out of my palm, and vowed to keep my temper. Pick her up at the end of the driveway? *Huh.* Run her over more than likely.

I counted to ten. Four times.

Still toying with the idea of vehicular manslaughter, I started the truck and aimed toward my aunt. The hat saved her. Titled over her left eye and looking as bedraggled as she, the hat seemed more pitiful than comical, and my aunt more vulnerable than annoying.

If nothing else, she's teeny. Not more than five-foot-one and pint-sized, Aunt Amy's heavyweight personality always overpowered her lightweight appearance. As I was growing up, she seemed so intimidating, so overshadowing. She has been described with such hefty adjectives as charismatic, outspoken, principled, crazy, and self-righteous. Her unconventional antics were called quirky, eccentric, and even deranged by those of us who love her, as well as her detractors.

Suddenly her autocratic idiosyncrasies seemed a bit foolish, and the power of her physical presence diminished. Not that she was feeble or entirely feeble-minded. Not yet, anyway. Just fragile. Her body as well as her intellect, and possibly her confidence. Until this moment, I had always thought of my aunt as invincible. I now accepted that she might be failing. Our family's redoubtable loose cannon might not be as indestructible as she wanted to appear.

As I watched her struggling to keep her balance on the uneven driveway skirt, I was struck by the fact that she might be struggling even harder to maintain her dignity — well, her version of it. What had sustained her throughout her entire life as her vivid individuality (her description), now appeared more like the foolish antics of a crotchety, slightly daft curmudgeon. Her trademark moral certitude could be seen as bordering on cranky arrogance, and her strong-minded behavior simply stubborn self-will.

With those disconcerting thoughts nudging my heartstrings, I knew that today would not be the day that I ran her over. Maybe tomorrow. Sensing the shift in the emotional climate, Aunt Amy begrudgingly allowed me to help her into the truck. And I'm pretty sure she gave my hand a little squeeze before slapping it away.

It is more than slightly ironic that I let her run roughshod over me on a regular basis. As my students know, I don't usually take much guff. I figure if I don't give it out, I won't get it back.

"I mean seriously, Ms. Marshall, we respect you. Besides, you don't even need to yell. You've got that hairy eyeball thing down pat. You could outstare Medusa." I took this with a grain of complimentary salt coming from Rory Cheff, eighth grade whiz kid and wisenheimer who never seemed particularly intimidated by my relatively ineffectual schoolmarm glare. My highly-touted Medusa stare didn't slow him down one iota the time I caught him and his partner in crime, Bill Carmish, hacking into the school's Learn to Type program.

"*Nothing*, Ms. Marshall. We're not doing anything. Just typing stuff for our science fair project. Here, take a look."

I looked at the computer screen. All I saw was a perfectly respectable bibliography. Disliking the "I'm totally innocent" gleam in his eye, I shot him a "I know you're up to something" glower right back.

"*What*? It's a bibliography. What's the problem?"

"The problem, Rory, is that Mrs. Luffman says lesson one instructed her fourth graders to type 'ass, lass's ass, ass, lad's ass, ass—'"

"And you have a *haunch* we're *behind* it, Ms. Marshall?" he punned with a barely suppressed snicker.

Sigh.

"Lesson two instructed them to type 'kiss ass, glad ass, sad ass'; you get the idea."

"You gotta admire the thematic consistency," Bill offered with a smug smile.

Cutting his eyes at his fellow hacker, Rory added, "It wasn't *us*! If Mrs. Luffman is going through the roof, it's her own *ass*phalt."

Rory sniggered. Bill looked perplexed. "Get it, Bill? Ass-phalt," prompted Rory.

ACK ATTACK

He got it. "Oh. Ass-uredly!"

It's hard to frown convincingly while stifling a laugh.

Neither jokester would have confessed if I hadn't overheard them bragging about their prank later that afternoon. Hairy eyeballs had nothing to do with extracting their confession.

"Gotcha! To the office with you both," I commanded when I caught them tooting their own horns.

"An ass-ignation with the Ass-istant Principal I ass-ume?" Rory asked. The kid just doesn't know when to quit sometimes.

The boys fixed the typing program, Bernice Luffman's students learned the first two keyboarding lessons in record time, and only four irate parents called the office. While I got credit for the bust and an unearned boost to my tough teacher reputation, my don't-mess-with-me repute does not impress Aunt Amy in the least. She's been bossing me around since forever and she's not likely to stop now.

Hoping that Chloe and Jackie would remember that Shad needed their cars as well as their extra

90

hands for the move, I set off toward her apartment over Island Pharmacy. After turning off Cliff and heading down North Liberty, we passed Sunset Hill and the sign for the Oldest House. "*Romeo and Juliet*. It's that kind of story," blurted Aunt Amy.

"*What* is what kind of story?"

"The house. The Oldest House is that kind of story. Young lovers. Feuding families. Shakespeare."

My look of confusion was deliberately misinterpreted as an invitation for an explanation. Delighted that she had once again opened the door for a random monologue about Nantucket's history, Aunt Amy proceeded to tell the story of the Oldest House.

"Hats. Two beaver hats and thirty pounds sterling. That's what the original settlers agreed to pay Thomas Mayhew for Nantucket—1659 it was. A hat for him and one for his wife," instructed my aunt. I pieced together that the original ten settlers, known as the first proprietors, granted themselves complete control of the island government by issuing themselves each a full-share vote, and then settled in to start a textile industry and enjoy life as gentleman farmers.

"Hopeless. Those full-share men were hopeless. Conditions on this island couldn't possibly support a textile industry; and they couldn't build a boat, make a rope, or catch a fish.. Had to import some blue collar workers for the grunt work." The imported skilled artisans were enticed to settle on Nantucket with a promise of a half-share ownership in the settlement and half of a vote in the local government.

"Half-share, half a vote. Those ten full-share rascals outvoted the fourteen half-share men every time," she offered as clarification. It appears that with their limited voting rights, the half-share men were never able to flex their political muscles, and soon began demanding equity in the settlement's government. Evidently, these unmet demands soon boiled into a feud known as the Half-share Revolt which, though acrimonious and long-lived, never escalated to actual bloodshed.

"In 1681 that scalawag Tristram Coffin, leader of the full-share faction, up and died. John Gardner, the leader of the half-share faction, was ready to make peace," she continued. "Gardner's daughter, Mary, had fallen in love with Coffin's grandson, Jethro, and the young lovers, you know, like Romeo and Juliet, had pledged to marry. Bad blood be damned!"

Apparently, I did not react with a suitably dazzled ah, ha! expression. "See? There you have it—young lovers, feuding families; Shakespeare," she related.

Without pausing for a breath, she charged ahead with the rest of the story. The Garners and the Coffins were more tolerant than the Capulets and the Montagues and wisely opted to accept the inevitable; in 1686, they built the young couple a house as a wedding present. The land was donated by the Gardners, the lumber came from the Coffins, and the old quarrels were momentarily put aside.

"The Nantucket Historical Association owns it today. It's a museum, you know. The Oldest House, the Jethro Coffin House—same thing. Don't know why they call it Jethro's house; he was hardly ever there; always off tending to his logging business on the mainland. Should call it the *Mary* Coffin house. She gave birth to at least six of her eight children right there in that very house. Raised them there, too—practically singlehandedly."

Somehow Aunt Amy concluded her jumbled history lesson back at the beginning. "See? Shakespeare, only without bloodshed and suicides."

Before I had a chance to respond, she bolted off on another tangent. "Lily Pond. Bet you don't know why they call that marsh over there Lily Pond when there isn't even a pond there," she quizzed, pointing toward the grassy Lank Bank park on the left.

Knowing full well that if I wasn't careful, another muddled history lesson was on the way, I lied. "Yep. I know that one."

Undeterred, she explained. "It *used* to be a pond in the 1600s — a three-acre one with boats and a man-made ditch connecting it to the harbor — before that Love Paddock came along."

It took her most of the trip to Shad's apartment to unravel the story. As I understood it, Love Paddock was a young girl who, according to legend, was responsible for the 1720 disappearance of the pond. "The world's first eco-terrorist," pronounced Aunt Amy.

It seems that Lily Pond, originally called Wesco Pond, was the site of a fulling mill and a place where Love Paddock enjoyed playing. One day while playing near the dam, she innocently dug a hole in its wall with a shell. Enjoying the trickling water,

Love resumed playing and didn't think to patch the small hole when she went home. By morning, the pond was empty and the boats were beached. Poor Love Paddock was too scared to confess.

The enraged islanders blamed the act on any number of hoodlums, misfits, and ne'er-do-wells. The public outcry was so intense that Love Paddock kept her guilty secret until just before she died.

"Speaking of secrets," I interrupted, hoping to waylay another befuddled monologue, "did you hear about Jennifer Krause? Gary's wife? The one with the big hair? I heard that she tried to kill him — with a pair of scissors!"

"Jennifer and Gary Krause? Not surprised. Those two have been united in holy *ac*rimony for the last fifteen years. One of 'em was sure to take a *stab* at the other sooner or later," she giggled. Without a pause, she crowed, "Puns. Two puns and you didn't get either of them!"

Ugh. Had she been hanging out with Rory?

"Acrimony, stab, scissors; got 'em," I countered, successfully stifling a sardonic groan and forging ahead with my verbal detour. "According to the grapevine, Jennifer's a long-time druggie. Been hooked on heroin for years."

"A-ha! Pre*medi*cated murder!" she joked.

As the budding comedienne guffawed at her latest one-liner, my phone rang. She snatched it from my purse before I even considered whether to pick it up, and answered with a shoddy imitation of my usual hello. Grinning like a snake, she covered the phone and stage whispered, "The best person in all the world is calling you."

The best person in all the world could only be David Malenga, her knight in shining armor. The man who single-handedly saved her from "the long and crooked arm of the law."

"Oh, David," Aunt Amy simpered in "my" voice, "I was hoping that you and I — "

My turn to snatch the phone. While tucking it between my left ear and shoulder, I heard David's playful, "Why, Mrs. Delano, how lucky for Maggie that you are helping her find her voice."

"Very funny, David," I broke in with my signature gravely bark.

"You might want to take a page or two from your aunt's book; a little syrupy simper and a touch of the come-hither," he added lightly in a tone that under different circumstances I might have interpreted as wistful.

"Are you downtown or at Island Pharmacy?" I asked, quickly changing the subject and hoping that some member of my family was not once again taxing his seemingly limitless patience.

"I'm at Island Pharmacy, and that's why I'm calling. Shad got here early and started her move without you. It seems that she's gotten herself wedged in the back stairwell. She's—"

"Hurt?" I interrupted, instantly imagining dire catastrophe. "Hurt?" I repeated anxiously, right over David's reassurance.

"No, no, relax. She's fine. Just a bit jammed up," he quipped.

Finally taking a breath, I asked what had happened. Shad, who is even more impatient than I, had begun to move her stuff without us. Characteristically, she started with her most prized possession—the most prized *and* the heaviest.

ACK ATTACK

"I'm not sure what happened," David began. "I heard a huge thud, a muffled grunt, and enough swearing to warrant a quick look-see. What I saw was an upside down dresser wedged in the crook of the stairwell. What I heard coming from behind the dresser was undoubtedly Shad. Her command over the blasphemous is quite impressive."

I knew just what dresser he meant. It was a marble-topped beauty that Shad's great aunt Marie had given her for her eighteenth birthday. Heavy as lead. A family heirloom and a treasured reminder of her deceased great aunt, the dresser followed Shad wherever she went. We shuffled it in the spring; we shuffled it in the fall. Along with the dresser, we moved boxes and boxes of Aunt Marie's hand-me-downs. Thimbles, goblets, china figurines, snuff boxes, finger bowls, vintage clothing, and candlesticks. Cartons full of the stuff. Twice a year.

"Once the cussing died down, I was able to get the gist of what happened," he continued. "Shad had turned the dresser upside down and was easing it down one stair tread at a time. As she was rounding the corner to the second landing, her cell phone rang. Unlike her mother," he added pointedly, "she couldn't resist answering it."

"Damn phones," I muttered.

98

"It seems that when she tried to reach her phone, she lost her grip on the dresser. The dresser slid sideways and Shad was wedged between it and the wall." With an amused chuckle he continued, "Stuck in the corner, she didn't have enough room to go up or down, reach her phone, or push the dresser away from her."

Having summarized as best he could how Shad had managed to imprison herself on his staircase, David suggested, "I think we can move the dresser, if we can get someone on the other side of it to push."

I was trying to visualize how this someone was going to get to the other side of a well lodged, bow-fronted, two hundred pound dresser, when David added, "I think there is enough room for someone to crawl through the legs of the dresser. There isn't much space, but you might fit. If not you, then surely your aunt."

Trying *not* to imagine a scenario that included my aunt, I thanked David and added, "We're on Pleasant Street now. We'll be right there."

"No rush," he ribbed. "I don't think Shad's going anywhere."

"Well?" urged my aunt as I closed the phone. "Is she all right? What's going on? What happened? Why did David call? Why didn't Shad —?"

"She's fine, Aunt Amy. Fine. Just slow down."

"*I'm* not driving. *You* are. *You* slow down."

I swear she says things like that on purpose, just to be contrary. The model of dutiful niece, I filled her in on what had happened. Without one snarky remark. Moments later we pulled into the parking lot behind David's pharmacy. At nearly the same time, Jackie's silver, bumper-stickered Escape braked into the slot next to mine. Type A Chloe was already parked by the dumpster, busy texting where-are-you messages to Brett, no doubt.

Before I had turned off the motor, Aunt Amy swung open the door and plopped down to the macadam. With a slight wince, she secured her balance, patted her ridiculous hat back to center, and tottered vampishly toward Jackie's car. Turning on the charm, the would-be vixen oozed, "Well, well, well. Boston, my main man. Delighted to see you again."

Great.

CHAPTER 7 — The Dirt on David

Boston. Another unpleasant surprise to add to the day.

He sidled up to Aunt Amy, took her hand, affected a courtly bow, and planted a courtier's kiss smack dab in the center of it. "Hell-*loooo*, Mrs. D," he schmoozed as he proceeded to tuck her arm under his and escort her regally toward the shade.

The shade, coincidentally, was about as far from the epicenter of the pending work as one could get and still seem to be in the work zone. Once in the shade, they performed their usual ritual: a complicated handshake involving multiple high fives, a couple of knuckle knocks, various thumb contortions, a left and right hip bump, and a melodramatic hand slide.

Ugh.

My first impulse was to toss her royal highness back into the truck and seal the doors. My second thoughts, slightly less extreme, prevailed. There was no doubt that we were all a great deal safer if Aunt Amy was out of the way, and somehow Boston would manage to avoid helping anyway. Flirting and jiving kept them both out of my hair. With those thoughts dropping the blood pressure a notch, I elected to ignore them. They'd both get my exasperated two cents sometime later that day.

David, who was just coming out of the side door of the pharmacy, must have witnessed most of their ridiculous antics. "Ah, the rescue team arrives," he ribbed without bothering to hide his mocking grin.

Carrying a fold-up chair and a copy of the Sunday *New York Times*, David followed the happy couple to the shade, seated my aunt, and offered her the paper. Distracted from her tomfoolery with Boston, Aunt Amy was temporarily neutralized and out of harm's way.

Irked that he was no longer the center of anyone's attention, Boston plugged in his ear buds, cranked up the volume, and sang along to "Raised in the Hood" — almost on key, but not quite. He can out-dance Michael Jackson, but he can't sing worth a hoot. Not that he seems to notice; his unprompted performances are frequent, loud, and generally accomplish his attention-seeking goal. If you count "Oh, shut *up*, Boston!" as getting attention.

"Thanks, David," I said as I strode past him. "Shad? Shad? Are you all right?" I bellowed up the stairwell. Unable to understand what she was saying from behind her wooden barricade, I forged ahead. "David, can you give me a leg up?"

"An arm, a leg, whatever," he responded drolly, hoisting me up between the dresser's legs. Feeling a bit like one of Cinderella's big-footed stepsisters, I scrabbled and pulled while David hoisted and pushed.

"This might not work," I muttered from the underside of the dresser.

"It's working for me," said David as he administered a totally unnecessary and rather spank-like push to my behind.

I gave one last effort to squish myself into the far too narrow opening. "You aren't going to like this," he began, tugging me backwards by the belt loops, "but we need your aunt. Her shoulders will fit; yours won't. We need to try it."

"Nope. No. Not. We are not stuffing her under a dresser."

"I'll get her!" Evidently Jackie had followed us up the stairs and was gung-ho to stuff Aunt Amy. She was none too happy with her frolicking with Boston; I didn't imagine that she was too happy that he encouraged it, either. She eagerly hurried off to fetch the would-be harlot and have a few words with Boston. Probably not the congenial kind.

As Jackie arrived with Aunt Amy in tow, her cell phone rang. It was the hospital; two patients had just been admitted to the ER. One was a burn victim and the other was a child having seizures. She passed my aunt unceremoniously to David and hollered, "Boston, I gotta go. Can you drop me at the hospital?"

Sensing that he had just found a way to avoid some unpleasant afternoon drudgery, Boston grinned, gave a mock salute, and hastily climbed in behind the wheel of the Escape. No one expected him to come back.

"Mom? Mom?" came Shad's rather pitiful, echoing voice from behind the mahogany bulkhead in the stairwell corner. "Do you think you ought to call the fire department or something?"

The choice between a rescue by Aunt Amy and a rescue by the fire department should have been quite simple. However, *The Inquirer and Mirror* often sends a photographer and a reporter to tag along with dispatched rescue teams. I did *not* want another front-page shot of me or my family doing something absurd. Last week's close-up of Aunt Amy in her Legalize Marijuana T-shirt winning the karaoke contest at the Chicken Box was enough for one month.

"David," crooned my aunt, taking his arm and batting her eyes, "come to rescue the Delanos again?"

"Why, Mrs. Delano," charmed David, "I believe we are going to wriggle again."

Chloe's laugh cut short whatever inappropriate reply Aunt Amy was about to make. With a sly, collaborative grin at David, she added, "Brett's on his way; he got caught in rotary traffic. Some fool went the wrong way, tried to back up, and crashed into a tour bus." Wasting no time, she continued. "Let's see if Aunt Amy will fit."

Another eager stuffer.

Enjoying the limelight, Aunt Amy handed me her hat, smoothed down her hair, and took a deep breath. "Shad! Here I come, Shad!" she added dramatically.

I imagined a muffled, "Oh, no," from behind the dresser.

As David hoisted her up, Aunt Amy's head and shoulders disappeared into the tiny space.

"The A-Team is here. No, wait — the *double* A-Team." Chuckle, chuckle. "The Amy-Ann Team." With a heralding "Ta-da!" a magician would envy, she disappeared piece by piece — white linen shirt, Murray's Nantucket Red belt, madras shorts, knobby knees, skinny calves, and pom-pom socks. The Keds vanished last.

We heard a solid thump, an "*Oooofff*," and a distant but clearly indignant, "I don't suppose anyone thought about what would happen when I got to the other side."

Aunt Amy had made it through.

"Are you all right, Mrs. Delano? Mrs. Delano?" David called.

"Concussion. A slight concussion. Nothing to worry about."

Feigning concern, David assured her that he would give her a thorough checkup once the dresser was out of the way. "Do you think you can push the dresser just a little bit to your right, Mrs. Delano? If you can move it just a few inches, I think I can get a grip on it and slide it back to center."

We heard an enthusiastic, "Pushing!" just before the dresser was solidly launched at least a foot to the right. "How's that?" she asked. "More? Say what? More?" Without waiting for a reply, Aunt Amy delivered another surprisingly exuberant double-leg push. The dresser began to teeter on the edge of the stair tread and slide toward us.

"No!"

"Whoa! Whoa!"

"Stop!"

While David braced the dresser with his shoulder, we helped slide it gingerly down the rest of the stairs. Shad, looking a bit wobbly and definitely teary-eyed, followed sheepishly along behind it. She had Aunt Amy's hand in hers, and it was difficult to tell who was supporting whom.

Once at the bottom, David ministered to my "concussed" aunt, and I hugged my daughter. Easily reassured, Shad was quickly back to her old self. Regrettably, once doctored, Aunt Amy was back to *her* old self. While Shad, Chloe, and I carted boxes down the stairs, my aunt flirted shamelessly with David.

"Willa Hornsby. Remember Willa, David?" she asked, escorted by David to her throne in the shade. "When she got that tick bite on her shoulder? My stars, if she didn't take off her blouse right in your pharmacy! Full of people, too. Said she wanted to make sure you saw the bulls-eye rash. My Aunt Fanny! What she *really* wanted...."

I didn't wait around to hear what Willa Hornsby *really* wanted from David, and joined the movers schlepping Shad's overflowing boxes. By the time Brett arrived, some of the furniture and most of the boxes had been loaded into the trucks. Since he had the good sense to arrive with coffee for all and

Downey Flake donuts, it was difficult to be cross with him. Eager to make up for his tardy arrival, he also did the lion's share of the remaining work.

Shad, despite her gypsy-like living, has accumulated an enormous amount of stuff: closets full of coats and hats from her great aunt Scotty; Victorian bric-a-brac from her grandmama; a lightship basket collection from my mom; and a great deal of heavy antique furniture from her great aunt Marie. All of this gets lugged, hauled, and dragged from place to place each spring and fall. "Honky rubbish," Boston calls it.

"Family heritage," counters the prickly Shad.

Heritage or rubbish, we had filled all three trucks. Mindful of the time, we hurriedly finished the donuts, glugged the coffees, and thanked David for helping us once again.

"And I promise I'll pay for any damage," said Shad as she collected Aunt Amy's hat from me, helped her to balance it on her head, and settled her onto the front seat of my truck.

I lagged back to thank David one last time, and he asked with a sigh, "Do you think I could see you sometime *without* your family, *without* a catastrophe, and *without* incident?"

Taken aback and at an unusual loss for a smarty-pants remark, I stammered, "Uh-huh, sure," and tripped another unnecessary thanks over my tongue. Afraid I'd be caught blushing, I waved cavalierly and climbed into the truck. Worrying that I might seem ungrateful for his help or — worse yet — grateful for his invitation, I added yet another pointless, "Thank you."

"So, Mom," started Shad from the backseat of the truck, "what was that all about? Got anything you want to share with us? Are you going to see him?" she teased with a huge grin.

"Scared. She's too scared," decreed my aunt. Thinking she had said all that needed to be said on the subject, she handed Shad the newspaper and asked her to read some of the headlines aloud. "Can't see very well when I am in motion."

Although Shad knows perfectly well that Aunt Amy can't see very well under any circumstances, she elected to accept the face-saving white lie and humor her. While the two of them skimmed the

Times, I busied myself with a much-needed repair of my No Man Ever Again bulwarks.

It had been ten years since Shad's father and I had called it quits, and he had moved to the Cape with his new girlfriend; one would think that I would be ready for another relationship. However, I had learned the hard way that I was, by nature, far too tenderhearted, insecure, and vulnerable to try it again. Afraid to give my heart away, I walled it up instead. My boundaries have been well fortified by busyness and bossiness. My family obligations, my work schedule, my ever-ready flippant remarks, and ten years of patrolling my emotional perimeter have kept me risk-free and safe.

David, however, has a way of slipping through my Don't Trespass boundaries. A gentle, bespectacled bear, David is the heartthrob of the senior set. Not quite a senior himself, David nonetheless is gifted in the art of winning geriatric hearts. It could be his boyish good looks, his gentle humor, or his cheerful response to their every beck and call that has them all swooning. He delivers their medication, soothes their fears, and makes sure that their medical needs are tended. No wonder they adore him. My aunt, obviously, is no exception.

I've known David for years—he has been our family's pharmacist and friend for over thirty of them. He was with us at my uncle's bedside when he died. He made the arrangements when Chloe needed a medi-vac flight to Boston for an emergency appendectomy. He fought Medicare's red tape for Aunt Marie, got Aunt Scotty a power chair when she could no longer walk, and took care of Jackie's rabies shots after the pit bull attack.

For years my family has been trying to play matchmaker. Their well-intentioned efforts are so absurd that David seems as embarrassed about them as I am. They transparently manipulate seating arrangements at family dinners, repeatedly ask me to pick up their prescriptions, and frequently conspire to leave the two of us alone whenever possible. Left unchaperoned, David and I are then supposed to...well, I don't know what. Fall passionately into each other's arms, I guess.

Not at all comfortable with *that* thought, I tucked it away for later consideration and tuned into Shad's current events summary from the newspaper. "The GOP claims immigrants are taking minority jobs, half of the men in the United States have HPV infections, ex-Goldman executive charged with insider trading, Iraqi authorities uncover sarin gas stash, stock prices slide with renewed fear of Middle East unrest, Venezuelan union boss gets seven-year sentence for extortion...." recounted Shad.

"Stop! Enough! More than enough. Get me the crossword puzzle. Where's a pen?" Apparently my aunt was done with the news summation.

As she was rummaging on the floor for a pen, Shad's phone rang. Knowing that I would probably not answer *my* phone, Chloe had called on Shad's to suggest that we all come to her house for tonight's family dinner. Promising to pass along the news, Shad offered to bring sushi and volunteered me for salad and dessert. As usual, Jackie would bring the beverages and munchies, and David, always included in our family dinners, would bring a pasta dish. Hoping he would make my favorite, Pasta Denifrica, I relayed the info that I would also bring cheese and fruit.

"Four. Four mills. Did you know that there used to be four mills on this hill?" blurted Aunt Amy as we drove by the iconic Old Mill on Prospect Street.

Not suspecting that Aunt Amy was in docent mode, Shad inquired, "When was that? Where did they go?"

"Destroyed. Torn down. Exploded. Dismantled. Even the Old Mill was almost lost—sold for firewood. Twenty dollars. In 1828."

We then learned enough about that mill to get a job as a tour guide. Built in 1746 on Mill Hill—or Popsquatchet—today's well-known tourist attraction was then one of five working mills grinding corn for island farmers, whaling merchants, and dock workers. At that time, Nantucket's thriving whaling industry sustained a population of nearly ten thousand, roughly the equivalent of today's year-round population.

Without missing a beat, Aunt Amy outlined the history of the mill as well as the rise and fall of the whaling industry. It seemed that at the height of the whaling era, the mill ground more than a ton of corn a day. However, the Great Fire of 1846 destroyed the commercial wharves, the whaling enterprises on the docks, and most of Main Street, leaving economic ruin in its wake. In addition, a series of storms silted in the harbor, and New Bedford, with a much deeper harbor, replaced Nantucket as the whaling capital of the world. With the decline of the whaling industry, the demand for corn decreased dramatically and the unused mills fell into disrepair.

Sensing that she might be boring her eye-glazed audience of two, Aunt Amy added a couple of anecdotes to spice things up. She could not conjure up pirates, murders, or a resident mill ghost, but did offer that according to legend, the mill had played an important role in a spy network during the American Revolution. She explained that the miller would use the position of the canvases on the four vanes and the direction in which he pointed the top of the mill to secretly report on the strength of the British fleet in the harbor. Some even claimed that the British got wise to the treachery and had their warships fire cannon shots at the mill in retaliation.

"Poppycock. *That* story is pure poppycock, but Caroline Comstock's isn't," segued my aunt.

"Who is Caroline Comstock?" Shad asked, virtually guaranteeing another jumbled anecdote.

"Caroline Comstock. She and a friend were climbing on the vanes when a gust of wind came along. As the vanes started turning, the friend jumped off. Not Caroline Comstock—whooshed to the top, seventy feet up in the air. *Then* she let go. Fell to the ground in a crumpled heap, of course."

As Aunt Amy told it, there was no doctor available. Caroline was taken to the butcher's shop, wrapped tightly in animal skins, and survived, writing about the near-fatal ordeal in her journal many years later. "Which is more than I can say for the cow," she teased.

As expected, Shad asked, "What cow?"

"The dead one," was her unhelpful reply.

"All right, I'll bite. Which dead one?"

"The mill's dead one. The one that grazed too close to the mill, got walloped in the side by one of the vanes, knocked a few feet, and died. That one," concluded Aunt Amy.

"So, no ghosts, no pirates, no spying. Nothing but a dead cow?" I interjected, feeling slightly peevish.

"*And* a plunging girl," offered Shad to our deflated storyteller.

As my aunt was *harrumph*-ing her retort, we turned off Cliff onto Washing Pond Road. Hoping to forestall another re-telling of Aunt Amy's naming of Washing Pond and the early Quaker sheep industry story, I hinted, "Remember, Shad. Aunt

Amy has already told us how Washing Pond got its name."

Not to be denied the presence of a captive if unwilling audience, my aunt launched into the story for at least the fiftieth time. "Sheep. Washing Pond got its name from sheep. Washing Pond is one of the places where they washed the sheep before they sheared them." Just gaining steam, Aunt Amy continued, "Sheep shearings! What a time those Quakers had at those sheep shearing festivals. Why there was — "

"We're here, Aunt Amy," interrupted Shad. "Let me help you out. Want to lie down while we unload the trucks?"

Not a chance.

"I'll just go inside and wait on the couch for Boston. Said he was coming over later to teach me the words to Snoop Doggy's latest."

Something else to look forward to.

CHAPTER 8 — Bad Stuff at Tom Nevers

While Shad settled Aunt Amy and her newspaper on the couch, I palavered with Chloe and Brett. All agreed that there was no point in waiting for Boston to reappear and decided we had better just get going if we wanted to unload the trucks before lacrosse practice.

"How about if we unload your truck first, Maggie?" suggested Brett. "That way, if you and Shad need to leave, at least your truck will be empty. Chloe and I can finish up."

"Would you mind, Uncle Brett?" Shad asked. "I have to get my car, stop at Island Variety for water bottles, and gather all the team equipment from the Parks and Recreation office before practice — like, in an hour."

He didn't mind. In fact, he would do anything for Shad. Spoiling her even more than he spoiled

119

his own daughters, Brett's soft spot for Shad has been apparent her whole life. Brett never took his children anywhere without inviting Shad. Ski trips, sailing excursions, camping, or shopping, it didn't matter. She was always included.

Shad's feelings for her uncle were equally transparent. His name, Ba-Ba, was one of her first words; she was holding his hand when she took her first step; she chose him to drive her to her first day of kindergarten; and it was Brett she called when her first boyfriend broke her heart.

Chloe and I exchanged knowing grins, added our superfluous agreement to the proposed plan, and began stuffing all of Shad's worldly goods into her room and the adjacent spare bedroom. The overflow spilled out into the hallway and seeped into the living room—even into the kitchen. We saved the wretched dresser for last.

"I don't suppose you would consider leaving this behemoth here this fall? Maybe some of the bric-a-brac? The hats?" I asked hopefully.

"Nope." No elaboration. Just, "nope."

With all but a few boxes stashed, Shad announced, "Time to go, Ma!"

"Let me check on Aunt Amy. I'll be there in a sec," I responded as she kissed Brett's bearded cheek and hugged Chloe. "Hey, Chloe, if Aunt Amy's asleep, I'm *not* waking her. Check on her later, would you?"

"My turn, *eh*?"

"Yup," Shad and I replied in unison.

I confess to an ulterior motive. Although I wanted to make sure my aunt was sound asleep and now Chloe's responsibility, I also wanted to snag her newspaper. There was something about the sarin gas headline that was pricking my curiosity. Perhaps while Shad was running drills, I could read the full story.

Tiptoeing into the living room, I carefully approached the couch from behind. Although my snoozing aunt was collapsed on a corner of the paper, I was pretty certain I could ease it out from under her without waking her up.

Wrong.

Aunt Amy popped up instantly. "Ready. Time to go? Ready. Where's my hat?"

Rats.

ACK ATTACK

"Aunt Amy, *you* are not going anywhere. Shad and I are going to her lacrosse practice; you're staying here. We'll come back afterwards and pick you up in time for family dinner."

"Pee. I just have to pee. Meet you in the truck."

Knowing it was futile to argue, I accepted my fate and hoped my aunt would resume her nap on the ride out to the Tom Nevers fields. I retrieved her hat from the floor, quietly tucked the newspaper under my arm, and helped her up. Adjusting the hat took a bit longer.

"Front. It goes in front. Not there—to the right. Good. Now tilt it a little."

Chloe helped Aunt Amy get her bearings while Shad rummaged her lacrosse equipment out of the rubble heap on her bedroom floor. I grabbed some leftover morning coffee and dug last year's sunscreen from the depths of the drug drawer.

"Three of these prescriptions are expired, this antibiotic cream is older than most of your children, and the Tums are moldy," scolded David last week as he rooted through the drawer looking for a Band Aid. "What's wrong with the medicine cabinet in

122

the bathroom? Why a drawer in the kitchen? And what are these false Harpo glasses doing in here?"

"Distraction. Splinter removal distraction."

"Maggie, your kids are practically middle aged."

"Grandkids."

An audible sigh from the meticulously organized David.

While Chloe loaded Aunt Amy in the front seat, Shad climbed in back, and I secured the snagged newspaper under the stash of cloth grocery bags on the console. I dropped Shad at the pharmacy to pick up her car, offered to get the lacrosse equipment, and headed for the Parks and Recreation office at the Delta Fields. By the time I had pulled up to the equipment shed off Nobadeer Farm Road, Aunt Amy's thunderous snores assured me that she was enjoying a nap worthy of Rip Van Winkle. With luck, she would stay that way for a while.

The traffic on Milestone Road was light, so it was an easy drive out to Tom Nevers. An old naval station, Tom Nevers was used as a bombing range during World War II, and served as a submarine listening post in the fifties and a bomb shelter for JFK when he was president. Today, it serves the island in more mundane ways. In addition to the activities on the ball fields, beaches, and the playground, Tom Nevers huge open fields host the annual summer carnival as well as our Island Fair in the fall. The fall fair is my favorite.

Each September, when most of the tourists have gone, Nantucketers reconnect with each other and re-stake their claim to their island. They host an old-fashioned county fair with livestock shows, pie eating contests, kiosks for local crafts and produce, pony rides, apple bobbing, a pet show, and scarecrow making. The winning entry in the pumpkin growing contest is always the centerpiece of the festival. Last year's champion, a 742-pound warty giant, was displayed in front of the fire station until it rotted out just before Easter.

After pausing to appreciate the incredible views from Tom Nevers bluff, I turned onto the park's dirt road, followed it to the backside of the fields, and pulled into the most remote parking spot I could find. Hoping that remote would also ensure quiet, I crossed my fingers that Aunt Amy would sleep right through practice. Silently slipping out of the truck and closing the door with what I hoped was an inaudible click, I tiptoed toward the back to get the equipment.

"Awake. I'm awake. Help me down. Where's my hat?"

Reluctantly, I helped her out of the truck. Her hat, a little worse for the wear, was retrieved from the dust-coated debris on the floor in the back. I placed it just so on her head, adjusted the rather tattered veil, and secured it with a stray bobby pin she had found in the cup holder.

Just as we set off toward the practice fields, Cousin Elizabeth honk-honked her way past us. She pulled into a spot close to the pavilion, opened her door, and released chaos.

Four yowling beagles clamored over her lap and, with great hullabaloo, set their sights on Aunt Amy. Butch arrived first, claiming the honor of delivering the knock-down punch and pinning Aunt Amy to the ground. Quickly followed by Sundance, and finally Clyde and Bonnie, the dogs covered my happily squealing aunt in slobbery, gooey kisses.

"Babies! My babies!" gushed Aunt Amy as she tried to get her feet situated underneath her.

"Down. Down. Get down," shrieked Cousin Elizabeth, inciting the opposite effect.

Grabbing as many leaping collars as I could and administering a firm knee-block to Butch's chest, I grabbed Aunt Amy with my free hand and hollered at Elizabeth to call off the dogs. I added a few unprintable, dog-demeaning descriptors for emphasis as I snagged my aunt's hat from Clyde's drooling maw.

Aunt Amy might have spent the next blue moon on the ground if the dogs weren't so easily distracted. Spotting a bunch of sea gulls raiding the trash cans near the pavilion, the ADHD beagles yowled their *Braveheart* war cry and set off in pursuit.

"Pajamas. Aren't they just the cat's pajamas?" Aunt Amy cooed.

Since no comment was necessary, I gave Cousin Elizabeth the double whammy: a hairy eyeball *and* the schoolmarm tone. "Tag, you're it. Your turn. *You* watch her. And you'd better go get those dogs." As she bustled daintily off in the direction of the four beagles with Aunt Amy in tow, I tossed the hat in the front of the truck and stamped back to the tailgate to unload.

Shad pulled in just as I was getting the gear organized. We loaded it directly into her car and drove toward the practice field closest to the pavilion, which was also closest to the beagles, Cousin Elizabeth, and mayhem. Sea gulls were screeching, trash was flying, and Aunt Amy was down again.

"Oh, no. That's not who I think it is, is it?" Shad asked dispiritedly. "Cousin Bizzybreth and the Baskervilles," she correctly reckoned using our family's less-than-flattering nickname for the five of them.

Once again, no comment was necessary. "At least Cousin Elizabeth's in charge of Aunt Amy. We're off duty."

"Yeah, right," she said, watching my cousin's ineffectual efforts to control the dogs and get my aunt up off the ground. Again.

As we turned into the parking place, three chattering girls mobbed the truck.

"Coach!"

"Hey, Coach!"

ACK ATTACK

"Coach, can I help?"

Since another four or five equally animated, chatty girls quickly joined them, I figured they could take care of the gear while I took care of the parents, the lists, and the forms.

I should have stuck with the gear. Gear doesn't complain or whine. It also has no sense of entitlement.

"My daughter has been playing for the Baby Whaler team for years. I'm certain Coach will put her on the starting lineup."

"This is a ridiculous time to have practice. I've had to drop my Pilates class."

"My Cheryl was an all-star for the Mini-mites two years in a row. I expect that she will be made Captain."

"I don't see why we have to drive all the way out here. Coach should get us time on the Delta Fields. Under the lights would be perfect."

"I played center for U Mass in the NCAA nationals in 2001, and I've been coaching Missy ever since she could walk. I am sure she will be first string center."

I was getting a splitting headache.

Envious of Shad, who got to run off with the girls, I did my best to make non-committal responses to the crowing and griping, organize the forms, and distribute the lime green team shirts. Each overly doting mother assured me that her daughter had a well-fitted mouth guard, a proper stick, and regulation goggles.

Aunt Amy was with Cousin Elizabeth, and Shad was jogging a few warm-up laps with the girls. I was, for the time being, off duty. I headed for my truck with visions of a few solitary minutes to read the newspaper and maybe catch a power nap.

Ha.

Halfway there, I was flagged to a halt by Cousin Elizabeth's strident yelling and frantic waving. Despite the fact that she and Aunt Amy were on the other side of the field, I could sense some urgency in her summons.

So much for the newspaper and the nap.

I headed across the field with the enthusiasm of a heretic on the way to the stake. Noticing that one of the dogs — it looked like Sundance — was writhing on the ground, I quickened my pace.

It was Sundance, writhing and yelping while Aunt Amy wrung her hands and Cousin Elizabeth screamed, "Do something! Do something!"

I raced the last twenty yards and elbowed my way through the milling dogs and their panicked owners. I attempted to cradle Sundance's head, stroke her side, and speak as soothingly as I could. Before I could finish a cursory examination, the other three dogs, tired of simply milling about, bounded in to assist. Their clamoring, licking, and pouncing made any kind of examination impossible, but the rough-and-tumble play distracted Sundance from her thrashing.

As Sundance calmed down, I was able to see that she had burned her muzzle. The burned spots were clustered mostly around her mouth, but also dotted her jowls and nose, with a few on her upper torso. It looked as if Sundance had found a container filled with some extremely hot liquid or even some kind of acid. She must have bitten into it and picked it up to give it a playful full-body shake. The contents seared her mouth, splattered into her face, and splashed on her shoulders. The burns looked painful, but not too serious.

"Go get some ice water out of the cooler," I directed Cousin Elizabeth. "We've got to bathe her muzzle — rinse all the burned spots," I ordered, thinking out loud.

Cousin Elizabeth, Butch, Clyde, and Bonnie all went to fetch the ice water while Aunt Amy repeatedly demanded, "What happened? What happened?"

As I quieted Sundance and explained my theory, Aunt Amy began searching the ground for something that could hold such a dangerous substance.

"This? Could it have been this?" she asked, holding up the tattered remains of what appeared to be a carton. It wasn't a disposable coffee cup or one of those Styrofoam soup bowls. It was more papery, with black writing on the side — like the phosphorous ones I had found in the compost.

"*Ow! Ow! Ooowwww!*" she cried, flinging the container pieces to the ground. She waved her right hand in the air, swore like a truck driver, and stomped the container to beat the band.

We had found what had burned Sundance.

It didn't take long for Cousin Elizabeth and her unmanageable dogs to arrive with the ice water. We bathed Aunt Amy's hand and Sundance's burns while speculating on the presence of such a toxic substance at Tom Nevers *and* at the dump. The cold water baths were effective; our speculation was not.

A relatively subdued Cousin Elizabeth, surrounded by her roiling pack of mongrels, set off to get her car. We needed to get Aunt Amy and Sundance some real medical attention. With luck, Jackie would still be at the hospital and Bailey, the island's vet, would be able to take a look at Sundance.

"Family dinner's at Chloe's at six o'clock," I shouted after them.

After they left, I thoroughly searched the surrounding area. Sundance had probably picked up the container near the entrance to the old bomb shelter where I was standing. Starting at the boarded-over door, I carefully combed through the weeds and slowly worked my way out from the old entranceway. Although I picked up a good deal of litter, none of it was toxic. I double-checked the area, circled around to the back of the shelter's twenty-five foot mound, and searched that area as well as the area around the nearby deserted shed.

I was fairly certain that there were no more containers around. Trying to put aside my blossoming obsession with phosphorous containers, I gave up the search and joined Shad as she finished up some catch-and-throw drill and sent the girls on a water break.

"What was *that* all about?" she asked.

"Later," I said.

Shad went over to talk to the moms just as a freckled-faced, redheaded lass ran up, shook my hand, and boldly inquired if I was Coach's mother.

As the mother of Coach, I have a great deal of unearned prestige. Young players think that their coach walks on water. *Ipso facto*, the mother of the coach must be worthy of worship as well. I was not about to burst that bubble.

"So, tell me about Coach," insisted the redhead whose name turned out to be Sarah. "What bad things did she do when she was young? I bet she smoked pot. Did she have boyfriends? Did you ever catch them kissing? Doing other stuff? Hey, maybe *you'll* tell me about that other stuff. You know, where babies come from."

Oh, boy.

Sarah reminded me of Shad as a youngster. It served Coach right that she would have someone on her team who was as fiery as she was. Payback. Since there was no guarantee that Shad would have to raise a daughter quite as feisty as she was, Sarah would have to do for now.

"I'll tell you what, Sarah," I hedged. "I'll tell you about the time Shad stayed out all night and came home cross-eyed if you promise to ask *her* where babies come from—and make sure she answers you."

Correctly suspecting that Sarah and I might be up to no good, Shad blew her whistle, declared the water break over, and lined up the girls to take shots on the goal. I wasn't sure, but there was a good possibility that Coach sent a few squinty-eyed daggers my way.

I joined the gaggle of moms on the bleachers and watched the last twenty minutes of practice. With a final pep talk, sweaty hugs for all, and a reminder to meet at the field next Saturday at three o'clock, Shad sent them on their way.

In no time at all, we loaded up the few pieces of unclaimed equipment into the truck. I filled Shad in on what had happened to Sundance and Aunt Amy and told her I was going to call the hospital to see what was going on. Shad said she would pick up the fixings for family dinner and meet me back at the house.

Promising to call her as soon as I had news about Aunt Amy, I dialed Jackie's cell.

"Yup, she's here. I got her," Jackie answered without even so much as a hello.

Promising to fill me in on the details at family dinner, Jackie assured me that Aunt Amy was fine and asked me to remind Boston about dinner.

"And don't pull that 'Oh, I forgot to call him' routine like last time," she snapped.

Who me?

CHAPTER 9—The Dirt on 'Sconset

On my way to return the extra equipment, I called Shad to let her know that Aunt Amy was fine. To show her appreciation for my help at lacrosse practice, Shad had volunteered to get the groceries for the night's dinner. Since she was stuck in the Stop and Shop parking lot doing a bumper-to-bumper stalk for a place to park, she also agreed to call Cousin Elizabeth to check on Sundance. She did not, however, feel appreciative enough to call Boston. That was left to me.

After my third attempt to reach him, I gave up. He wasn't answering his phone, his voice mail was full, and I didn't want him to come to family dinner anyway. I decided I had done my sisterly duty; Jackie would surely disagree—not an unusual state of affairs when Boston was involved.

I mentally scrolled through my responsibilities for the rest of the day. Aunt Amy was with Jackie; Shad was getting the food and calling Cousin Elizabeth; Chloe and Brett were hosting the meal; David was bringing pasta; Jackie was bringing drinks and snacks. I was, for the present, free of family duties and ready to play hooky. Perhaps now I could read the paper, maybe take a quick drive into Siasconset for a cup of coffee, and drive by Hulbert Avenue to see what was going on there.

Instead of turning left toward home, I turned right toward 'Sconset, island shorthand for the cumbersome Siasconset. I passed the cranberry bogs and golf courses, and mindful of the bumper sticker admonishment, Twenty Is Plenty in 'Sconset, eased my way into the village proper. As I passed the old pump in the town square, I could almost hear my aunt recounting the history of this quaint fishing village and telling us stories about her girlhood summers there.

Like most of Nantucket, 'Sconset has changed a great deal, yet its essential character remains the same—peaceful, cozy, casual, intimate—a place for unwinding, centering, and just plain loafing. Originally a haphazard collection of fishermen's shacks, 'Sconset became a refuge for summer people who renovated, built, and restored, leaving tiny rose-covered cottages, gracious summer houses, and the basic shops and services for a relatively self-sufficient village. There has always been some sort of general store and a post office; and at various times a bookstore, a library, taverns, hotels, and a railroad connecting 'Sconset to the town of Nantucket.

Aunt Amy recalls tennis at the Casino, dinners at the Chanticleer, dances, baseball, movies, and most of all, walks on the beach. She paints colorful verbal pictures of the honey man selling his sticky wares from his pushcart; of the organ grinder and his frisky monkey; of the Dine A Mite Tea Room and the Kozy Beauty Studio. Her favorite stories often feature the tall tales told by the gentlemen members of The Srail Club, 'Sconset's equivalent of Nantucket's Wharf Rat Club. Since srail is liars spelled backward, Aunt Amy's outrageous Srail Club stories were our favorites.

We Marshall sisters have our own 'Sconset stories. They don't, however, involve tearooms or beauty parlors. Our stories feature beach parties, bonfires, all-night stargazing, fishing for blues, and weekend-long picnics. Thanks to her vigilant monitoring of the police band, Aunt Amy knows most of our stories.

Most, but not all.

We hope.

No need for her to know about the time Ned Coffin, Jackie's secret crush, stole our clothes from the shore while we were skinny dipping. Or the time we got Chloe's Jeep stuck in the sand at the turn of the tide and the onset of a brisk nor'easter. Despite our frantic shoveling, the Jeep was soon deep in the surf- waves crashing over the top of the hood. David had towed us out of that mess, and — come to think of it — had brought us towels after Ned's prank.

Chuckling at the memories, I scanned the area for a parking place near the 'Sconset Market. I was in luck — there was a space right in front of the building with plenty of room for my truck. Although my aunt still criticizes the "lily-livered islanders" who voted to lift Nantucket's ban on automobiles in 1918, most of the rest of us appreciate their decision. Despite the fact that our narrow side streets are choked with cars from June to September, our present day lifestyles depend on being able to get around the island easily.

Nantucket is not very big: three and a half miles wide and fourteen miles long. Consequently, we have all gotten accustomed to living in proximity to everything. I have often moaned, "What? All the way out there?" if I had to make a flower delivery out in Wauwinet—a grand total of about seven miles.

We have no traffic lights on the island. None.

Our only super highway is the Milestone Road, which connects the eastern end of the island with the town center. The speed limit is a blazing 45 mph.

Our Main Street is one-way and cobbled with stones that many believe were brought over from England as ballast in the cargo holds of the empty whalers. After off-loading their barrels of whale oil in England, the ship captains had to add weight to their vessels to safely make the return voyage to Nantucket. Supposedly Joseph Starbuck, a wealthy whaling merchant, used these cobblestones to pave the road from the wharves up to the top of Main Street, where he had built identical brick mansions for his three sons, Matthew, George, and William.

Captain Joseph Starbuck, who made his fortune in the whaling business, was not a whaling man. He was a whaling merchant. He had gone out whaling only once. That one trip was enough to assure him that whaling was 85 percent tedious sailing, 5 percent dangerous whale chasing, and 10 percent smelly blubber boiling. To keep his sons from doing it, he bribed them with houses, and all three elected to stay on Nantucket to run the family whaling business and live in their grand Main Street mansions.

Since it was the mid-1800s, Captain Starbuck was not about to build his daughter Eunice a mansion. Rather, he told her to go out and marry someone who could build her one. A dutiful daughter, she did just that. In 1822, Eunice married William Hadwen, who built her a bigger and better house right across the street from her three brothers. A wealthy whale oil and candle-making merchant, Hadwen built not one but two Greek Revival mansions — one for his wife and one for Mary Swain, his beloved niece.

Take that, Joseph Starbuck.

Grateful for the islanders who had lifted the ban on automobiles and lucky to have found a convenient parking place on Memorial Day weekend, I headed into the market for a cup of coffee. And maybe a double-dip Heath Bar Crunch ice cream cone.

"Ahhh, Maggie. I'm in luck. Twice today."

Ernie Whitehead. Twice in one day, lucky?

"And where is the redoubtable Amy Delano? Dog obedience training, by any chance?" He scoffed.

"No...um...at the Nobby Shop being fitted for the suit she'll wear to the White House. For the Appreciation Ceremony, you know," I lied.

"Well, the neighbors are going to express *their* appreciation for all the congestion and attention she has brought to the neighborhood. We're meeting next week to discuss passing a usage restriction ordinance to prevent her from letting that federal rabble into Brant Point again."

"Ernie," I ventured, "would you, by any chance, be singing a different tune if it was *your* house that was being occupied and you were the one being received at the White House?"

He was unwilling to concede an inch. "I wouldn't set foot in the White House while there was a taxaholic Democrat in residence. Count on it," he responded. "Besides, Justine Forrester heard that Mamie Bascomb read that there are a bunch of foreigners in Senator Marques's house. Towel Heads."

Sometimes there's no point in arguing with prejudice like that.

"See ya, Ernie." Not sure if my departure was a cowardly act of conflict avoidance or a laudable trip on the high road, I bit my tongue all the way out the door.

Once back in the truck, slopping ice cream on pages, I rooted through the paper to find the article about the sarin gas on page three. "Iraqi authorities uncover sarin gas stash...chemical weapons production facility...crude but effective equipment...huge stockpile of ingredients... concentrated phosphoric acids...volatile nerve agent...deadliest of toxic vapors...."

Yikes. Apparently with enough funding, a chemical weapons engineer, a source of ingredients, and some easily obtained equipment, any ole extremist could manufacture the lethal stuff. The article saved the relative good news for last. Getting the toxic chemicals from the lab onto the targeted victims is a much more difficult process.

In the past, terrorists have not been very effective with their delivery of sarin or any of the other lethal bio-agents like anthrax and Ebola. The most successful attack had been the 1995 sarin gas attack in the subways of Tokyo that left thirteen dead, many seriously injured, and thousands with vision problems. However, the information that radical extremists were continuing to stockpile deadly nerve agents and improve their methods of delivering them did not seem like very good news to me

"If you didn't cause it and you can't control it, detach," my wise ole mom told me more than once. I mentally heard the shortened version, "Detach," even more often. Since there did not seem to be any constructive act I could take toward thwarting attacks by bio-agents, detachment seemed to be my best option. I would even take detaching one step further: denial.

Not a fan of denial, my mom would have disapproved of my readiness to disregard the possibility of a biological attack. However, "Progress not perfection" was another of her favorite maxims, and I, doing the best I could, would rely on that one for the moment.

I have always found that some ideas are just too scary to think about when they are brand new.

I have usually needed a little denial to act as a shock absorber. Although I am more realistic than I used to be, I'm not sure that my progress has been as stellar as Mom might have hoped.

Mom had many other sayings from her twenty-eight years of AA sobriety. "First things first," "One step at a time," "Easy does it," all have become essential mantras in my daily living and the lives of Jackie and Chloe as well. We are caretakers by nature. It is extremely difficult for us to separate caring for others from taking care of things for them; helping others from rescuing them; supporting others from enabling them. I count on Mom's maxims to help me navigate all murky emotional waters.

Putting my worries about biological warfare in my cerebral Denial Box, I mopped up the sticky dribbles from my cone, restarted the truck, and decided to take the scenic route through 'Sconset. Heading down Baxter Road, I passed folks in the throes of opening their summer houses, sculpting their privet, and setting up for cookouts. Impressed with the industry of others, I proceeded to mosey my un-industrious way out to Sankaty Lighthouse to finish up my coffee.

I am one of many islanders with a bumper sticker that reads, I'm a Keeper. Besides the appeal of the self-affirmation in the literal message, I also want to be publicly counted among those who contributed to the effort of moving the lighthouse away from the edge of the eroding bluff.

The Siasconset Bluff has been vanishing at an alarming rate. Sometimes up to ten feet a year. Had it not been for the fundraising efforts of the 'Sconset Trust, our historic lighthouse—so old that it was originally used as a lookout point for off-shore whaling—would have fallen over the cliff.

Mentally applauding the efforts of preservation and conservation organizations, I turned back to Bayberry Lane and headed toward Quidnet, another old fishing village that has become a prestigious summer community. I passed by the exclusive Sankaty Golf Club (a mile-long waiting list to pay a king's ransom to join), then followed Polpis Road toward Quidnet and Sesachacha Pond. Pronounced "sach-ja-ka," this 280-acre pond has been, according to Aunt Amy, "Victimized. Abused. The victim of tree-huggers. Meddling, off-island, sanctimonious, boobocratic tree-huggers."

Islanders have a long-standing history of opening shoreline ponds to improve the fishing. Not only does it improve the quality of the fish harvest, but pond openings also control mosquitoes and cleanse the pond water. Despite these beneficial effects, the Massachusetts Wetlands Protection Act put an end to this practice in 1981. There has been controversy and illegal breaching ever since.

"Butt out. Those *federales* need to butt out. Mind their own damn business," Aunt Amy says frequently. "We can protect our island without any help from them."

I have to agree with her. Nantucket has an excellent track record. Through the years we have placed nearly half the island under various conservation restrictions. Even Jackie, who is a more ardent conservationist and a less patient niece than I am, agrees with Aunt Amy — and agreement between those two is rare. Usually when together, one or the other is in a huff of ruffled feathers, obstinately defending her position or resolutely attacking the other's.

After mentally adding an hour to my dashboard clock to adjust for Daylight Savings time, I realized that I was running late. If I wanted to drive by Hulbert and still get home in time to help Shad, I had better not tarry. Wondering for the zillionth time how to change my clock, I decided—as I have for the last twelve years—to just wait until fall when my clock would once again be accurate without subtracting the hour. Why do today what you can put off 'til tomorrow, and then not have to do at all? Another of my favorite maxims.

As I approached town, I called Chloe to see if there were any last-minute items she wanted me to pick up for her. Glad that she seemed to have everything under control and I wouldn't have to join the grocery store gridlock, I rounded the Milestone Rotary and turned onto Orange Street.

If Marine Home Center, our island's only true hardware store, had been opened, I would have been stuck in snarly traffic. Since it was Sunday and the store was closed, I traveled quickly down Orange, turned right on Union, and right again onto Washington. The light traffic flow allowed me to enjoy the view of the harbor up ahead. Many of the Figawi boats were still there and in full sail: jibing, tacking, and coming about as they jockeyed for position in the next race.

The town pier was crowded with boats, as well as their bustling, busy crews and gaggles of party-hearty spectators. The traffic, a mixed bag of autos, bicycles, mopeds, and pedestrians, congealed as I got closer to town. My snail-paced progress past Straight Wharf and the bottom of Main Street slowed to a mere creep as I approached Steamboat Wharf. The road was swarming with sunburned, travel weary day-trippers, impatient cars maneuvering for a spot on the next ferry, and tipsy bar patrons from the nearby restaurants partying in the street.

Driving in all that commotion reminded me of those video games the kids at school play all the time; the ones where obstacles appear out of nowhere, dash straight at you, miss you by a hair, then swirl and dodge all around. Half the people in front of me were oblivious to the traffic, the other half purposefully obstructing it.

"Cars. Not people. *Cars* are the problem. Ban 'em again," says Aunt Amy every time I grouse about tourists who treat Nantucket like a giant pedestrian mall.

"And just where would that leave *you*? Walking to the grocery store? I doubt it," I countered once.

"Hitchhiking."

I believed her.

When I turned onto North Beach by the yacht club, the kaleidoscopic movement of cars, bikes, and people diminished and the drive down Easton to the rotary became less challenging. I passed families loading mountains of beach paraphernalia into the backs of SUVs, stuffing coolers, kids, chairs, and neckerchiefed dogs into Land Rovers; and families on rented bikes weaving in and out of the all the hullabaloo. Most of the folks I passed would be nursing blistering sunburns tonight.

As I was turning into Hulbert, I nearly collided with a silver Escape screeching around the corner and accelerating hurriedly out into the rotary. Son of a gun — was that Jackie's car? I don't think there are many other silver Escapes with as many bumper stickers on them as Jackie has on hers. I couldn't miss War Is Not the Answer, Visualize World Peas, and Tea Parties Are for Girls with Imaginary Friends displayed on the driver's side door. I knew it was Jackie's car — with Boston behind the wheel shouting into his cell phone, spitting mad.

Odd that he would be in this neighborhood. Odder still was the sight of Frick and Frack, my old friends in black suits and dark glasses, glaring pointedly at the retreating car.

Worried that Boston had said or done something to provoke the interest of the Secret Service, I pulled up next to them and asked, "Is there a problem?"

"No problem, ma'am," said Frick curtly.

"Move along," said the even less friendly Frack just as his cell phone rang.

He quickly retrieved his phone from his pocket, turned his back to me, and hunched over it as if to ensure a more private conversation. I could clearly hear the angry words of the caller: "That's what I said. You're a thousand dollars short!" And there was no doubt about who the caller was; I would recognize that irate drawling voice anywhere. Boston.

I hoped that neither of them saw the look of shocked curiosity on my face. Not wanting to push my luck, I shrugged, waved cavalierly, and drove on by as nonchalantly as I could.

I would need Jackie and Chloe to help me sort this out.

CHAPTER 10—The Dirt at Family Dinner

Chloe's phone was busy. Probably talking with one of her daughters—most likely Chelsea, who was due to have her second child any day now.

Jackie wasn't answering her phone. Like me, Jackie believes that since she pays the phone bills, the phone should be available for *her* convenience, not the convenience of her callers. If it isn't convenient to answer it—which is most of the time—neither one of us will pick up. Unable to reach either by phone, I planned to corral them at family dinner. Until then I would worry the odd snippets of information like a Jack Russell with a gnarly bone, trying to connect the dots between Boston, Frick and Frack, $1,000, Senator Marques, and Aunt Amy.

In a hurry to enlist my sisters in the dot-connecting, I took the most direct route home. Up Cobble Hill, a shortcut to Sherburne Turnpike and out to Cliff. Just before Washing Pond Road, I spotted Cousin

Elizabeth and her four dogs at the old Tuppancy golf course. Now owned by the Conservation Foundation, the links have been converted into a sixty-two-acre, oceanfront, leash-free dog park.

Although there is a leash law on Nantucket, it is rarely observed and hardly ever enforced. Dogs roam, romp, rummage, and run at will on beaches, in neighborhoods, on trails. They hardly need a leash-free park. Nonetheless, the sanctioned freedom of a leash-free play area has created a subculture of dog owners like Cousin Elizabeth who frequent Tuppancy's. Like all mothers and nannies who regularly frequent a children's playground, these dog owners develop friendships, gossip about each other's dogs, and steadfastly maintain their dog's innocence whenever the predictable tussles occur.

Hoping Cousin Elizabeth would not see me, I accelerated toward home. Although I felt guilty for avoiding her, I just wasn't up to the inevitable long, drawn-out account of her trip to the vet. I could see the bandaged Sundance racing across the moors. She was fine. I was in a hurry.

The fog was rolling in. If it got any foggier, there would be some unhappy travelers stranded at the airport. Our summer mornings and evenings are often shrouded in fog, and Nantucket residents know that they need to book their summer flights for a time in the middle of the day.

Island residents stoically accept the fact that traveling to and from the island can be a challenge. In the summer, fog frequently closes the airports. If the airport is closed, travelers rush for the boats. The boats are soon booked to capacity, and folks are stuck.

In the winter, the winds regularly shut down the ferry service. When the boats are canceled, travelers rush for the airport. The flights are soon booked to capacity, and folks are stuck.

There's a lot of getting stuck on Nantucket.

Islanders commonly go to ridiculous lengths if they have to get off the island by a specific day or time. I once had to leave Nantucket on a Wednesday afternoon to make sure I could get to New York by Saturday morning. The forecasted nor'easter did in fact hit the island Wednesday night. No boats and no planes until Sunday. Had I not left the island four days ahead of time, I wouldn't have made my connecting flight to West Palm.

It seemed that Maushop might take pity on travelers tonight and only send in a light fog. Meteorologists be damned. It is the giant Maushop who is responsible for Nantucket's fog. Not only is he to blame for our fog, but also — according to native Wampanoag legend — for the very existence of the island itself.

Maushop was an enormous giant who lived on Martha's Vineyard in the time of the Ancient Ones. He provided for his wife and family with whales that he caught barehanded as he walked in the sea. One day, while out gathering whales, one of Maushop's moccasins filled with sand. Eager to get rid of the uncomfortable irritation, Maushop headed back to Martha's Vineyard, sat down at the water's edge, unlaced the moccasin, and emptied the chafing sand back into the sea.

Viola. The discarded sand formed the island of Nantucket.

After inadvertently creating some of the most valuable real estate in the United States, Maushop re-tied his moccasin and began to smoke his pipe. A gentle, contemplative giant, Maushop smoked for a while, and the gray clouds of smoke rolled out over the ocean. Maushop's swirling smoke is the fog that so often blankets the island, stranding travelers.

In a hurry to get home and impatient with the driveway ruts that were slowing me down, I did an abbreviated beep and waved as I went by Chloe's. Although she and Brett were out on the deck setting up for dinner, I was in too much of a rush to stop. Busy with dinner prep, neither would be able to take the time to connect any dots with me anyway. If my nose was accurate, Brett was grilling some of his family-famous burgers, which meant that Chloe was assembling her renowned potato salad (secret ingredient: tuna fish). Better they should cook now. We could talk later.

I didn't see Jackie's car in its usual spot by the flaming red trailer. Hoping she hadn't gotten tied up at the hospital, I optimistically called her cell phone one more time. No answer.

Shad was home; I would use her as my immediate sounding board. Maybe she could help me by offering a fresh perspective. Perhaps what my burgeoning worries needed was a dose of cold water and a little common sense. I might have been overreacting, which is a habit of mine, so I am told.

"There's not a moderate bone in your body," David tells me often. "You're like Pop Rocks—instant crackle."

"Mom! It's me. Me, me, me," I greeted Shad.

When she was just a toddler, Shad began to announce her presence that way each and every time she came into the house. Whether she had been at day care all morning or out in the yard for a mere five minutes, the announcement was the same. "Mom! It's me. Me, me, me."

At some point in her post-adolescent life, I started to announce my presence that way to her. That tradition has become a mother/daughter ritual that seems silly on the outside but feels important on the inside.

Shad was up to her elbows in sticky rice and stinky salmon. Not wishing to join her condition, I settled for her "Hey, Ma!" and an air kiss.

As she finished rolling the sushi, I started making the salad and filling her in on the Boston, Frick and Frack, $1,000, Senator Marques, and Aunt Amy conundrum. As expected, her no-nonsense practicality put these events in a different light.

"You can't be sure it was Boston on the phone and you can't know why Frick and Frack were glaring at the car. Probably Boston said something crass as he drove by and he's lucky they didn't shoot him.

"And, Aunt Amy is not involved," she continued. "The Secret Service is only staying at her house to protect the senator and whoever is there with him. Granted, it sounds like there's a swarm of agents, but if there are Muslims staying in the same neighborhood as Ernie Whitehead, it's probably a good idea."

Good point.

Shad carried the trays of sushi and the platter of cheese and fruit. I grabbed the salad. We spent the two-minute walk to Chloe's catching up on news about Shad's three siblings—The Sibs, as she calls them. Jack and his wife were expecting their first child and were toying with the decidedly odd name Zephyr Lee for whichever gender popped out. Phil and his family had gone camping in Maryland's Susquehanna State Park, and Stan had taken his crew to Splashdown Fun Town in Vermont for the weekend.

ACK ATTACK

An aunt six times over, Shad was crazy about her nieces and nephews and kept in close touch with all of them. Their frequent texting, Facebook postings, and phone calls gave her rich insight into their day-to-day lives.

Shad gave me a quick update on my oldest grandson Jimmy, who had been suspended from school on Thursday. Apparently, while the girls' gym class was outside, he and two friends snuck into their locker room and rifled through the lockers, collecting all the underwear they could find. Stuffing their booty in an equipment bag, the boys then carried the loot to the boys' locker room for redistribution into those lockers. Quite taken with their own prank, they soon forgot about whispering. The coach, hearing the poorly muffled ruckus, caught them red-handed- arms full of bras, thongs, and camisoles; lingerie strewn everywhere.

Phil, Jimmy's dad, had done far worse things when he was in high school. He grounded Jimmy anyway. Not for the prank, but for getting caught.

"You will do plenty of foolish things. Just don't do them foolishly," Phil advised Jimmy as he passed the sentence: grounded for two weeks and no arguments.

As the eldest, Phil is the self-styled patriarch of the four Sibs. He taught his youngest brother Jack how to navigate the world of girls; bailed Stan out of more tight spots than I wanted to think about; and gave Liz her nickname Shad, short for Shadow. As she shadowed her oldest brother, Shad not only earned her nickname, but also learned some important lessons about compassion, perseverance, and loyalty. Phil has taught his siblings well. A tight foursome, my children trust each other implicitly. They share each other's lives, help raise each other's children, and only rarely gang up on me.

David's car was pulling in just as we got to Chloe's. He had changed out of his stuffy pharmacist suit and was wearing his ratty ole green sweater with what appeared to be new jeans. Nice and snug ones. Umm....

Yikes. Stop. Don't even think of going there.

Changing my focus to above-the-waist, I noticed that David had brought a huge bowl of Pasta Denifrica and a bottle of my favorite Riesling wine. "Yup. Just for you," he said as he swooped the bowl and the wine in front of me.

Before I could stammer out something inane, Jackie, who must have been sitting on the back deck, appeared with Aunt Amy trailing after her no-nonsense wake.

"Where's your car?" Shad and I asked in tandem.

"Don't even ask. Well, you can ask, but I don't know. Boston has it. He didn't come pick me up at the hospital, and he won't answer any of my calls," she fumed.

Oh, goody. Trouble in paradise.

Never missing an opportunity to add fuel to that fire, I added, "I think I saw him driving down by Aunt Amy's just about ten minutes ago—talking on his cell phone."

"Where's my phone?" she asked no one in particular as she turned on her heels and aimed for the back porch.

"*Oooooeee!*" said Aunt Amy. "She's been fuming all afternoon. On the way to the hospital, Boston said something about returning to Mississippi. Then he didn't show to pick her up after her shift. She had to call Josh and that trollop to come pick us up from the hospital. So I told her—"

Possibly in the hopes of curtailing a lengthy replay of the entire conversation and getting something to eat before it was cold, David cut in with a solicitous, "Ladies, may escort you in?"

As I hoped, there were burgers and potato salad. And the Pasta Denifrica. A carbohydrate addict's dream.

Over dinner, I spelled out my many worries and ticked off my few facts.

"I have another piece to add to the puzzle," said Jackie between bites of salad. "You know that burn victim at the ER today? Well, he had severe burns on his both of his hands," she began as she took a huge bite of her bacon and onion burger.

Chew. Chew. Swallow. Swallow.

"Jackie!" I said impatiently- tapping my foot, sighing exaggeratedly.

"Let the poor woman eat," David said soothingly as he filled my wine glass for the third time and patted me gently on the thigh.

The thigh?

Jackie paused between bites. "The burn victim, Aziz Hadad, had the same type of burns Aunt Amy has. Both of them were burned by a highly concentrated phosphorous substance. Aunt Amy's burns are fairly minor, but Hadad's were quite extensive. He must have had physical contact with a great deal of the stuff."

We all started talking at once, asking questions nobody heard, voicing opinions no one listened to, proposing theories that made no sense.

"Hold on, hold on," said David ineffectively. *"Hold on!"*

The last was loud and forceful enough to penetrate the din. Aunt Amy quickly cut into the hush that followed. "Burger. Can someone cut my burger? I can't do anything with this blasted bandage on my hand."

Not usually one to complain, she sounded kind of whiney. She might have been feeling a bit miffed that all our talk of phosphorous did not prompt a single one of us to ask about *her* burns. Or maybe she was just tired. After all, she's ninety — and, possibly, a mere mortal.

"At your service, Mrs. Delano," said David. "Wouldn't want you to go hungry in the middle of a meal."

"Let's just stick to the facts," said the take-charge Shad. "Just what we know to be true. No conjecture or assumptions, and one person talks at a time."

"Sumbitch," began Aunt Amy. "*I* know that phosphorous can burn like a sumbitch *and* there's some out at Tom Nevers. *And* I also know – "

"And someone disposed of a lot of phosphorous containers at the dump," I interrupted. "And, somebody thinks Frack owes him a thousand dollars, and – "

"And," Jackie interrupted, "at least one other person has received severe burns from phosphorous." She paused. Overdramatically, I thought. "What I haven't had a chance to tell you guys is that the burn victim, Hadad, was one of the three Scowly-faced guys we saw at Cy's last night."

Another hubbub of questioning and fruitless projecting.

"Pooped. I am pooped!" roared Aunt Amy over the commotion.

"May I drive you home?" inquired David with a pipe-down look at the rest of us. "Maggie, while your aunt gets her jacket, may I see you in the kitchen?"

Uh-oh.

Backed up against the counter in what I hoped looked like an offhand pose, I borrowed a page from Napoleon and decided the best defense was a spirited offense. "What?"

Spirited offense?

"Maggie, I imagine that this is not the time or place. I am also certain that there will never *be* a right time and place. So, it's now or never."

Gulp.

"Next Saturday, we are going out to dinner. You and me. Without anyone else. No sisters for backup, no aunt for diversion. Just you. And me."

"Ready. I'm ready!" Bless Aunt Amy for barging in just in the nick of time.

Barely masking a sigh, he lip-synced, "Next Saturday. No excuses." He offered his arm to Aunt Amy and, as the screen door slammed behind him, added, "Tell Chloe to just hang onto the pasta bowl. I'll pick it up tomorrow."

I quickly fled to the safety of the back deck. The same discussion was in progress, only louder and more heatedly. Brett was making stabbing motions with his fork to emphasize a point that Jackie apparently wasn't getting. Shad was enumerating her points on her fingers to Chloe who was shaking her head vehemently in disagreement.

"OK. Enough!" I decreed. "Let's do the dishes and talk about something else."

"I'll help, but then I've gotta go. My shift starts in an hour," said Shad. "Hey, why don't you guys come in for the island trivia contest tonight? That'll give you something else to talk about. Too bad Aunt Amy left—you'd wrap it up with her on your team."

"I'll drive!" said the ever-ready Jackie.

CHAPTER 11 — Dirty Doings at Trivia Night

"Wait! Damn it, I can't drive. I don't have my car," groused Jackie.

Chloe volunteered. "I'll drive. You guys go get ready; I want to call Chelsea first anyway. Pick you up in about ten minutes."

"I'll just get a heavier fleece and walk back," I said, relieved that I wasn't the designated driver two nights in a row. Maybe I wasn't the only one who had noticed the two refills of Riesling. Geez, David.

Brett was settling on the couch when I returned. A beer in one hand and *In the Heart of the Sea* in the other, he told me to send his regrets to Shad and keep an eye on Jackie. "She's still steaming. Always worrisome."

Remembering only too well Jackie's heated confrontations with officious bureaucrats at town meetings, her Save Our Sound picket lines in front of the post office, and the shouting match with the oleaginous health inspector that was captured by our local Plum TV, I promised Brett that I would do my best.

We both knew that my best was no match for Jackie's worst. Her full-blast tirades are as feared as her good works are appreciated. My mealy-mouthed cowardice in the face of confrontation is as legendary as my sarcasm. Smart-assed remarks? No problem. A real-life, adult-style assertive confrontation? Not a chance.

Jackie came out of her back door dressed in the same black jeans; a new, rather low-cut blouse; and a sporty cable knit cardigan. Her hair was out of the ponytail and, with a little help from the fog, at its frowziest.

Chloe gawked. "Is that makeup she's wearing? And dangly earrings?"

Chloe, who never wore anything but dangly earrings and wouldn't leave the safety of her house without her makeup in good repair, expressed what we both feared. "She is looking for Boston to make nice. Or she's looking for Boston to make trouble."

170

"Either way would make for nothing *but* trouble," I chimed in. "Let's hope he's holed up somewhere with his buddies. It's reggae night at The Muse; maybe he's there."

Jackie climbed in back, dove into her gargantuan Everything Bag purse, and pulled out a small thermos of water "I think David was trying to get you drunk," she said, handing me the thermos. "Are you ever going to drop your guard and let that guy through? Everyone knows he's been crazy about you since forever."

"No. Not happening. No," I pronounced. "Not interested. Nope. David and I are just friends," I blithered, not sounding at all convinced or convincing. Worried that one of them would taunt "Methinks she doth protest too much," I switched the conversational focus. "And, since *you* started the conversation about boyfriends, is it true that Boston's going back to Mississippi?" I probably sounded as hopeful as I felt.

That did it. Fury unleashed, Jackie raged about Boston the whole ride into town, and didn't stop until we had parked in front of the Hub. "Says he's leaving on the early boat on Wednesday. Had the nerve to ask me to pay for the boat ticket for his car. A one-way ticket, no less!" After a futile calm-down breath, she carried on. "I'd like to rip out his other eye!"

I'd always been curious about his missing eye. Hoping to assuage my small-minded curiosity and steer Jackie toward a less volatile topic, I ventured, "So, what happened to his other eye? Where did it go?"

"It didn't *go* anywhere," she snarled. "It was gouged out when he intervened in this mugging in New Bedford two winters ago. An elderly couple."

Intervened?

Mugger or mugee?

Not wanting to see us tangle or try to referee a squabble, Chloe chirped, "Let's see if the Cobbletones are singing on Main Street before we go to Cy's."

We had just missed the Cobbletone's last a cappella song for the evening, but town was still hopping. Rowdy celebrants surged and swelled in the streets; overserved revelers crowded the sidewalks; clusters of unrepentant smokers filled doorways.

Most of the swarms were wearing turquoise plastic Figawi bracelets; they'd probably just come from the awards ceremony over on New Whale Lane.

"Oh, jeez! She's gonna break her damn-fool neck," I said, pointing to a tottering, stilettoed matron trying to negotiate the cobbled street.

"Serve her right," said the still-piqued Jackie.

Just as it appeared Ms. Stiletto's torpedo-shaped body would topple for sure, her escort caught up to her, took her arm, and got her steadied. He must have been her husband, and both were surely tourists. No self-respecting islander would attempt to parade around Main Street in stiletto heels; or in his case a lime green ascot, pink whale-dotted pants, patchwork madras jacket, and white tasseled loafers — no socks.

"Hope they aren't going to Cy's," I remarked.

They were.

Entering just ahead of us, they barged peremptorily past the host and made straight for the last available table. We would have to settle for the stools at the counter between the bar and the dining area. At least the height of the stools gave us a full view of the entire restaurant so we could size up the competition for the trivia contest.

A quick perusal of the restaurant revealed none other than Ernie Whitehead. He was flanked by Justine Forrester, who wore a hempy, drab olive turtleneck; and Mamie Bascom in her signature neon-bright Lily Pulitzer. Unbelievably, they were intently studying stacks of hand-scribbled notes and carefully ordering a pack of three-by-five cards. Justine was thumbing through a manly handful of crib notes, quizzing Ernie, and brusquely correcting each of his responses. Tittering into her hankie, Mamie was fanning note cards out on the tabletop, rearranging, reassembling, re-sequencing.

Hoping to catch Alec's eye and place our order, I caught Ernie's eye instead. He sneered derisively across the tables between us. "Three times in one day. My, oh my. And no Amy-Ann to help the team?"

Pretending I was a grown-up, I settled for a wave with a half-hearted smile in his direction, as Alec, Shad's friend and co-worker, made his way through the mob to our table. "Hey, Maggie; girls," he said, flashing a grin that has broken many a heart. "What can I get you lovely ladies tonight? Wine? Maybe a Cosmo? Or perhaps — "

"Excuse me, young man! Excuse me. We were here first. We're ready to order," barged Lime Green Ascot. Dripping disdain, he persisted, "A Brandy Alexander for my wife, and I'll have a double scotch on the rocks."

Not nice to hope that Shad would spit in their drinks.

A seasoned restaurant veteran and well skilled at dealing with the overly entitled, Alec glanced their way, pasted a lips-only smile on his face, and responded, "Coming right up."

Ascot and Stiletto got a no holds barred, unabashedly mean-spirited People Poking. By the time we had finished with them, they would have been arrested if even half of it had been true: pedophilia; S&M; Ponzi schemes; meager IQs; grasping; ugly children....

Just as we were about to turn our Poking to the other bar patrons, tonight's emcee for the trivia contest stepped to the mike. Shad.

"Protest!" shouted Ernie suddenly. "Protest! Favoritism. Nepotism. The emcee is Maggie's daughter—disqualify them. I most surely protest!"

Alec, who was also a bouncer at the Rose and Crown during the week, spoke quietly to Ernie. Red in the face, Ernie kept any further protests to himself. More than a few people clapped.

Shad reviewed the rules: one minute to write down your answer; all correct responses receive a point; the team with the most points at the end of the twenty questions wins $100.

Planning to keep our brains well lubricated with Whale's Tail Pale Ale, we were ready.

Bring it, Ernie, bring it.

We got the first two answers easily. Not surprisingly, Ernie's team did too. Unexpectedly, so did the Ascots. *Hunh.* How did they know that the *Rose* was the first whaling ship built on Nantucket; or that in the whaling heyday of the nineteenth century, Nantucket was the third largest city in Massachusetts?

No one knew the next question. Why would anyone even make note of the fact that the Red Men's Club—originally the old Friend's Meeting House—had stood where the Dreamland is today? We glared at Shad, who shrugged as if to say, "I didn't write 'em, I only read 'em."

Justine Forrester snooted haughtily, Ernie scowled, and Mamie Bascom shuffled note cards under the table.

Note cards? Were they cheating?

The next three questions were a breeze for all of us. Even the Ascots, on their second round of drinks and an additional order of calamari, got the answers immediately. All twelve teams knew that widow's walks were originally used as staging platforms to put out chimney fires. Early colonists dumped buckets of sand down burning chimneys long before any Nantucketer went to sea in a whaling ship. The teams also knew that the Great Fire was in 1846 and that Maria Mitchell discovered her comet from the top of the Pacific National Bank.

The next question, however, eliminated five of the other teams.

"What were the names of the two Nantucket ships that participated in the Boston Tea Party?" asked Shad in her best Alex Trebek voice.

Only Ernie's team, the Ascots, the Marshall sisters, and two other teams knew the correct answer: the *Beaver* and the *Dartmouth*.

The next two questions were tough. Stumped by the fact that lower Main Street was once called State Street and that Herman Melville based *Moby Dick* on the sinking of Nantucket's *Essex*, two other teams fell by the wayside. Only three teams were left: the Marshalls, the Ernies, and the Ascots.

Bless you, Aunt Amy, for all those unappreciated history lessons.

Reassessing the competition, I alerted Jackie and Chloe to the possibility that Ernie's team was cheating. Something was fishy about the Ascots, too, but I couldn't put my finger on it. How did they know so much about the island? Just who were they? They were dressed like tourists, drinking like fish, and acting like they owned the place. What was their deal and how on earth could they eat so much? Alec was just serving them chicken quesadillas, an order of buffalo wings, and two bacon cheeseburgers — and another round of drinks.

Three teams. One last question.

"What is the highest point on the island?" boomed Shad theatrically.

"*Psst!*" hissed Chloe, jerking her head toward Stiletto. "She's putting the food in her purse."

Just as I was about to respond to Chloe, I saw Ernie look down at the note cards under his table then whisper to Mamie, the team's scribe. Ascot had seen it, too.

"Focus on the game, would ya?" coached the overly competitive Jackie.

Right. The clock was ticking.

We were pretty sure that all three teams would have the same answer that we did: Altar Rock. In fact, it seemed too easy. *Everyone* knows that Altar Rock is the highest point on Nantucket.

Wrong.

Apparently, Folger Hill, which I had never even heard of, was one foot higher.

The Ascots missed it. The Marshalls missed it. Ernie's team did not.

Shad gave me a don't-shoot-the-messenger grin.

"Cheat! Cheat! Cheater!" yowled Ascot, pointing at Ernie. "Show those cards, immediately!"

Wide-eyed and attempting to arrange an innocent look on his weasel face, Ernie held up his empty hands. "Sir, I protest my innocence and am appalled by your accusation!"

Because Ernie kept glancing guiltily at the floor, even the faraway Shad could see Mamie's fancy footwork as she dragged the abandoned note cards over to Justine. Pretending to scratch her puffy ankle, Justine was stuffing the cards in her wooly socks.

"Hey, Ernie—" Shad began just as the Ascots slipped from their seats and started easing toward the door — without paying their bill *and* with enough purse-stashed food for a week's worth of dinners.

"*Phweeeeet!*" Jackie has one of those piercing, fingers-to-mouth whistles.

Both she and Chloe were pointing to the escaping Ascots. I stayed focused on Ernie and the card-stuffing Justine.

Justine and Ernie, grateful for the diversion, stood up and pointed to the accelerating Ascots. "Quick! They're getting away!"

The milling crowd, mostly unaware of the drama unfolding, slowed the Ascots' hasty departure to a virtual halt. Just as Alec collared Ascot's patchwork madras jacket, Ernie demanded his prize.

"We won, fair and square. We want our hundred dollars."

"Won?" screeched Stiletto, whirling to point at Ernie. "*You* cheated. Give me those cards."

As the commotion threatened to worsen, Shad called into the microphone. "Ladies and gentlemen, that concludes tonight's Trivia Contest. Congratulations to our winners, the—"

Click. The mike went dead. Judging by the twinkle in Shad's eye, I was guessing that there might have been more to the click than electrical failure.

Alec escorted both Ernie and Ascot out of the bar. Justine, Mamie, and Stiletto trailed dispiritedly behind. I hoped Ascot would have to pay his tab. Ernie would pay with bad karma.

Grateful to have avoided an even more tumultuous scene and glad that Shad and Alec had restored order so quickly, I suggested that we call it a night. Although Jackie was somewhat reluctant, Chloe's reminder that they had planned to bike out to Wauwinet at seven o'clock the next morning convinced her.

Alec was swamped, so I made my way to the bar to pay our tab and say goodnight to our quick-thinking emcee. Just as I turned back toward the counter to collect my sisters, I spotted the last people I ever expected to see again: the three scowly-faced guys. They were seated way in the back corner, nearly hidden behind the row of amplifiers. One of the Scowlies had well-bandaged hands, and someone very familiar was walking their way.

182

Wait—was that Boston who just bumped into Scowly Number One? And did Scowly Number Two just pass him an envelope?

Jackie had seen it, too. With a flip of her frowsy hair and a downward tug at her already plunging neckline, she headed straight for Boston.

Uh-oh.

Chloe was hot on Jackie's heels. I rushed after them both.

Just as Jackie elbowed her way within grabbing distance of Boston's arm, two red-faced, staggering gents singing a slurry chorus of "Danny Boy" weaved between them. Taking advantage of the moment, Boston fled out the side exit.

CHAPTER 12—The Down and Dirty Debrief

"He's just not worth it, Jackie," I said, catching up to her as she was about to plow murderously out the exit. "Definitely not worth it."

"Amen," agreed Chloe as she caught up to us. "And anyway, your top two buttons have come undone. Come on, let's get outta here."

Restoring order to the front of her blouse, Jackie sighed. "You're right; I know it. Uncle, uncle, uncle. I give up. He's not worth it."

She looked so deflated. Heartbroken. Hugs, pats, and sympathetic nothings did little to brighten her spirits.

"Oh, come on. I can't be this pitiful in *public*. Let's go to my house. I'll put on a pot of tea. Supposed to work for the lovesick and downtrodden."

The crowds on Main Street had finally thinned out. Only those with the heartiest of livers were still carousing. The teams in the race back to Hyannis tomorrow morning may have been thinking of their 9:30 start time. An early night generally makes the transition to morning a bit smoother. So I'm told, at any rate. After a certain age, one's sleep patterns become so sporadic, "early" and "late" tend to lose any definitive character.

The shops were closed, and the bars were in the drudging final push to closing time. We drove down Federal Street, hooked the right by the Town Building, and then the left out by North Water Street to Cliff. A couple of the guesthouses still had lights on, and a handful of guests were still milling around outside the Century House. Nonetheless, the town felt like it was wrapping itself up for the night, and I was hoping I would soon be doing the same.

I considered it a hopeful sign that Jackie put on the kettle for a pot of Sleepytime tea instead of opening the usual bottle of wine. I rummaged in the spice cupboard for the honey, and Chloe found some poorly hidden chocolate — the universal cure for whatever ails you. Way better than tea.

"I guess I should have known all along what a crumbum Boston is," lamented Jackie. She was so miserable that neither of us was even tempted to add an, "I told you so."

"I know, I know," she said, sparing us prolonged self-censorship, "you guys have been trying to tell me from the get-go. I just couldn't see it—or maybe I did see it and decided I would rather be happy than right."

"I'm not sure you were really *happy*, Jackie." I hated to say it, but as long as we were being honest, I was going the whole nine yards. "Maybe you were just in love with being in love. You know what I mean? All that tingly fervor."

"Seems like you were looking for love where it wasn't going to be found, then just stayed in love with being in love to be in love," added Chloe with the convoluted, esoteric wisdom of a Zen master.

I don't know if it was the frank sisterly sharing, the tea, or the chocolate, but we soon had exhausted Jackie's angst and were feeling the tug of sleep.

"Before you guys go, would you help me lug Boston's stuff out of the living room? I just can't face the thought of seeing it first thing in the morning," yawned Jackie. "We can put it in the laundry room, and he can pick it up when he brings back my car."

Chloe gathered up a pile of musty clothes, and Jackie collected the CDs, DVDs, and shoes. I started picking up the tools: a drill, duct tape, assorted metal fasteners, coils of wire, pliers. There were switch plates; a rusty hammer; boxes of nails; a grungy, paint-spattered tool belt, and — oh my! — an empty white container. It was metal-lined, with familiar black writing on the front.

Phosphorous, written right on the label. Clear as a bell.

I summoned my sisters. "Boston may be a whole lot yuckier than we thought."

So much for bedtime.

We opened the previously bypassed wine, reopened the bag of chocolates, and began jumping to some pretty scary conclusions about Boston, the envelope, the Scowlies, and Frick and Frack. We couldn't really figure out any sensible connection between them; a lot of wild speculation, but nothing really reasonable.

It was way too late for these mental gymnastics. We agreed to shelve our guesswork until tomorrow when we could add a few level heads to the brainstorming. Shad, Brett, and David would surely have some rational explanation for the irrational fact that Boston was toting a phosphorous container around, had furtively received an envelope from Scowly Number Two, and had run like a fugitive when he saw us approaching him.

We sketched our plans for the coming day and agreed to meet for breakfast at Fog Island Cafe after Chloe and Jackie's bike ride. A family beach picnic at Hulbert seemed like a good way to end the holiday weekend. We split up the calls: I got Aunt Amy, Chloe got Cousin Elizabeth, and Jackie got Josh and Grace. I guess it went without saying that I would call David.

The picnic would be BYOE—Bring Your Own Everything. We could probably shanghai Aunt Amy's grill from her porch without getting shot and then heft it down to the beach. I had some hot dogs in the freezer, and I talked Chloe into making her baked beans. Jackie said she'd probably just bring sandwiches. Cousin Elizabeth would bring enough food for an entire Third World nation, and Aunt Amy would bring her white Zinfandel. Sounded like a good start.

"I'll walk down the hill with you," said Chloe, giving Jackie a final squeeze. "Got a flashlight we can borrow?"

Jackie's Everything Bag yielded not one, but two flashlights. Both were little rubbery jungle animals that shone their lights out of their mouths when you clicked them open.

Only Jackie. I smiled.

The fog had settled thickly near the ground, so Chloe and I made our way carefully down the path. The overgrown bayberry bushes and blackberry vines were in need of a thorough whacking. During the summer, the frequent traffic on the path kept the trail pretty clear. In the blustery winter, we manufacture feeble excuses to drive rather than to walk to each other's houses, and nature reclaims her territory. I made a mental note to bring up my industrial-weight clippers tomorrow.

Midway down the path, we stopped to say goodnight to our parents. Both of them had always told us that they wanted to be cremated when they died; however, they died together in a car crash before they had specified what they wanted us to do with their ashes. Without the need to carry out any of their wishes, we chose to satisfy our own.

We buried both sets of ashes in the setback area between the three houses. As long as the property stayed intact, no one could ever build in that spot. Their ashes were safe, and we enjoyed the comfort of having our parents close by.

A few days after the funeral, Chloe, Jackie, and I cleared away the surrounding brush and planted a garden, filled with the flowers and herbs Mom had always had in her kitchen garden: Bee Balm for tea and potpourris; sage and yarrow for fevers; anise, fennel, golden rod, and marjoram; Blue Cohosh, pansies, and hyssop for bronchitis; lemon balm and mint. The plants were good for what ailed the body; our "cemetery" was good for what ailed the soul.

Shad wasn't home yet. At the bottom of the hill, Chloe and I exchanged sleepy hugs. I turned to the right toward the boardwalk path to my back door, and Chloe went left. I could see Brett's silhouette in the kitchen doorway, waiting for his sweetie to come home.

As always, my back door, like my front door, was unlocked. Although David often tries to convince me otherwise, I feel completely safe leaving my doors unlocked on Nantucket. He reminds me that the Nantucket of today is not the Nantucket of my rose-tinted past. He even had an alarm system installed in the house. "For crying out loud, you live out here in the middle of nowhere. All by yourself half the time," he argues. "Anything could happen, and no one would know."

I have never set the alarm. Never. Not even once.

Despite my fatigue, sleep was slow to come. Elizabeth Berg's *Pull of the Moon* and another cup of herbal tea didn't quite do the trick. Mulling over the events of the day, the suspicions about Boston, and my concern for Jackie made it difficult to fall asleep.

"Mom. It's me. Me, me, me."

Shad was home and whispering the traditional greeting, as well as snuggling into a goodnight hug.

"Happy dreams."

"You too."

When I awoke in the morning, I felt far more refreshed than I had thought I would. I wondered if Jackie had slept at all. Sleep or no sleep, she wouldn't miss the bike ride with Chloe—or let Chloe miss it either, for that matter.

Jackie has given up trying to get me back on a bike. Since I broke my wrist on our last bicycle debacle, I wasn't about to try my luck again. Despite all the pressure to get back in the saddle right after you fall, I was resolute. I got all the exercise I needed in my gardens and didn't want to risk another six-week stint in a palm-to-elbow cast.

Shuffling into the kitchen, I noticed that Shad had propped a note on the coffee pot

> Check on me at 11:00?
> Make sure I'm up?
> TX
> I am loving you.
>
> P.S. That couple in the bar? Scam artists!!! Last weekend they won $200 at the Chicken Box (Name That Tune Contest) and walked out on a $378 tab with a purse full of food.
> P.P.S. I'll love you forever if you could go out to Tom Nevers for me. I left the dang clipboard (you know, the blue one, Save Our Sound sticker on the back) on the bleachers. I'll owe you one. OK, I'll owe you two.
>
> P.P.P.S. And I'll make you broccoli slaw.

The Ascots? Scam artists, *eh*? I had sensed something wasn't right. I hoped that they had to make good on their tab at the Chicken Box as well as the one at Cy's. Sometimes it's almost a shame that our modern legal system is based on justice and mercy instead of old-time revenge and retaliation. Seems to me that anyone who stiffs a restaurant tab deserves an eye for an eye consequence. Maybe just let the hard-working servers have at them.

A peek out the kitchen window told me Jackie's car was back. So was Boston's truck. *Hmmmm...*was that good news or bad? In an hour or so, she and Chloe would be setting out for their ride. I could catch up with them at breakfast afterwards. Get the scoop from Jackie then.

As the coffee brewed, I answered Shad's note.

> I'll get your clipboard, but you owe me
> three markers. And, broccoli slaw.
> Family dinner's a picnic at the beach
> in front of Aunt Amy's. If you bring
> 7-layer dip, then I'll wipe the slate
> clean. No markers owed, just slaw.
>
> I am loving you 2.

Savoring the brewing aroma of The Bean's special espresso roast, I grabbed my extra large mug and stared impatiently at the coffee pot. David was an early riser; I'd take the coward's way out and text him his invite to tonight's picnic. That way, I wouldn't have to actually talk to him. By the time I had crafted and sent my oh-so-blasé invite, the coffee was ready. Steaming mug in hand, I headed for the computer.

Surely if I scoured the Internet, I could find out more about what was going on at Aunt Amy's house. I was still convinced that there was some connection between Boston and Frick and Frack. Although there was no tangible evidence of the suspected connection, my instincts were raising red flags left and right. It's like when there is an office romance that the lovebirds want to keep secret: they are very careful to avoid doing anything to indicate that they are mad for one another, but without fail, everyone knows anyway. Ricocheting pheromones or raging animal magnetism or...something. Hard to hide something like that—whatever it is.

Well, in my mind, whatever it was between Boston and the security guys, it was something unsavory. I was sure Frick and Frack were glaring at Boston for a real reason. And I was equally sure that he was the one who had called Frack. If he had called Frack demanding $1,000, perhaps the envelope that Scowly Number Two passed to him in the bar last night had the $1,000 in it.

If any of that were true, then there was some sort of link between Boston, the two Secret Service agents, the money, and the three Scowly-faced guys. In addition, Boston and Scowly Number Three also had connections to containers holding dangerous concentrations of phosphorous.

I feared that Aunt Amy's house somehow might be in the middle of this mess. Well, the middle of the mess was probably what was happening at Senator Marques's house, not Aunt Amy's. Her next-door home was just being used to house the Secret Service. That meant it was housing Frick and Frack as well, and I didn't trust either one of them. Of course, I might not be very objective. They had, after all, gone out of their way to be downright rude to me. Twice.

What in the world did we do before browsing? In no time at all, my computer search had gathered all sorts of vague references to some top-secret negotiations between the Pakistanis, the Iraqis, the OPEC cartel, and the United States. Two of the sources speculated that the meeting was taking place at a remote spot on Cape Cod. Another source pinpointed Nantucket as the meeting spot.

I was pretty sure that I could pinpoint the spot even more accurately than the newsies. I was sure that the meeting was taking place at Senator Marques's house. With the festive frenzy of Memorial Day weekend and the whirl of Figawi Weekend, Nantucketers (and the world at large) might fail to notice the comings and goings of high-level diplomats and their cumbersome entourages.

If I was reckoning correctly, Frick and Frack were posted to secure the safety and secrecy of some pretty important stuff. According to one source, the Pakistani chief of state, the secretary general of OPEC, Iraqi President Nuri Mahmud, and our own secretary of state were probably at Senator Marques's right now. Quite an impressive array of muckety-mucks.

What was Boston doing lurking about in that scene?

Not wanting to jump on that mental merry-go-round without my second cup of coffee, I switched gears to scroll through my e-mail. There was one from David. Marked with a red flag:

I MEANT IT. SATURDAY NIGHT.
NO EXCUSES.
I'LL PICK YOU UP AT 6:15.
DITCH THE JEANS. WE'RE GOING TO THE GALLEY.

Better get that second cup of coffee.

Just as I refilled my mug, I heard Jackie's signature whistle. They must be ready to go.

Helmeted and spandexed, the two looked ready to take on Lance Armstrong. Jackie's sunglasses were probably hiding some pretty dark circles, but her spirits seemed determinedly light. Showing Chloe the latest three pictures texted by her son Heath, she had her game face in place and her worries well masked.

Heath, a new father, was out of control in love with fatherhood and with his son. Every day, up to five times a day, he sent his mom—the proud grandma—a picture of Connick in a different outfit along with a commentary on the sleeping, eating, and execratory habits of his newborn son.

Jackie was thrilled each and every time. She excitedly forwarded these pictures to the rest of us with added and rather lengthy elaborations on her grandson's latest accomplishments. We were initially tickled; now we couldn't wait for Heath's paternity leave to end. One picture a day would be just fine, thanks. And really, just how many exciting developmental challenges can a four-week old surmount on any given day?

Chloe informed us that Chelsea was on the trampoline in her backyard, hoping to induce her own labor. She had vacuumed the entire house, gone on the stair stepper in the basement for a half an hour, and raked up the accumulation of winter debris in the side yard. No luck. No water breaking, no contractions. Surely the trampoline would do it.

Obviously, Chelsea was another one burdened with the well-known Marshall patience.

As I watched my sisters peddling, swerving, and fishtailing their way out the sandy, pot-holed driveway, I decided that although it was early, I would call my boys. My sons are early risers like I am; maybe I could catch up with them before they got too busy with their daytimes.

Phil was finishing up a yoga routine in some wooded glen with his wife, step-daughter, and two-year-old grandson, Zack. Apparently, he was grateful for the opportunity to skip the meditative breathing part at the end of the routine and settled himself on the living room couch to give me a lengthy account of his son Jimmy's latest adventures.

As I learned while parenting Phil, grounding a child is only as effective as your willingness to guard the doors. And the windows. I was never very invested in the prison guard role, and Phil took frequent advantage. In fact, I think he probably did more things with his friends *while* he was grounded just to have the added pleasure of sneaking out to do them.

Jimmy was well-armed with his father's tricks. He also had the added bonus of instant communication. A couple of texts, and in a flash, a horde of friends was available to assist with a jailbreak.

Caught in the act of shimmying down the drainpipe, Jimmy was now in cyber prison, too. In addition to being grounded for two weeks, there would be no phone, no computer, and no iPad. Ouch.

My third son Jack and his wife Lynde were just pulling into the midwife's driveway to attend, as he put it, huffer-puffer coaching. He couldn't talk now, but he'd call me after. They were thinking of changing the name Zephyr Lee to Bobby Lee and wanted my thoughts.

I doubted they wanted anything to do with my real thoughts.

Stan regaled me with tales about the bravery of his kids at Splashdown Funtown. Every single ride, without hesitation—a great improvement for his formerly timid daughter. Par for the course for his devil-may-care, fearless son.

Running short of procrastination ploys, I headed to the gardens.

Crash! Smash! Bash! All from Jackie's house.

Not good.

With a sigh and a good bit of trepidation, I turned to head up the hill to see what was going on.

Jackie's back door slammed. Boston's truck door slammed. Boston was leaving.

CHAPTER 13 — Trashed

I knew I had better continue on up to Jackie's and investigate the smashing and crashing. At least I wouldn't have to face Boston. Slam, slam, and he'd flown the coop.

And just where was he *going* in such an all-fired hurry?

Despite the hinge-splitting slam, the back door was ajar. Entering somewhat cautiously into the back hall, I encountered nothing more menacing than a crusty sock. Crumpled food wrappings, a soggy pizza crust, and a barely legible note were on the kitchen counter.

It's been real, Babe.
The B.man

Jackie had housed, fed, clothed, and defended the schmuck for nearly a year.

It's been real?

I almost wished I hadn't walked into the living room. Boston had far too effectively added destructive injury to his insulting note.

Mom had fussed over a houseful of antiques all her grown-up life. She had gotten these antiques from her mom, my grandma Mampsie, who had gotten them from her mom. The crown jewel of all these matriarchal antiques was the floor-to-ceiling Chippendale desk with intricate, diamond-paned windows.

When the time came to settle our parents' estate and divide the antiques, we drew straws to see which one of us would take our pick first. Jackie got the long straw and chose the desk; Chloe and I threw in the matching chair and the side tables as a part of her pick. The chair had always been at the desk, and the two side tables had always sat on either side for as long as any of us could remember.

Over twenty-five years ago, Jackie had set them up that same way in her house. They were not that way any longer. The chair and tables had been reduced to kindling. The entire front of the desk was baseball-bat smashed. Glass shards and wood splinters covered the desktop and the surrounding floor; most of the shelves inside were broken or cracked. Exquisite Old World craftsmanship in smithereens.

A few pieces of Grandpa Cor's priceless ivory collection were left askew on the two undamaged shelves. The rest had been hurled against the wall or out the now-shattered front window.

Bastard.

As I set about picking up the debris, sorting what might be saved, and bagging what was beyond hope, I called David—and immediately burst into tears.

"Damn it! How could he?" I wailed. "Boston's trashed Jackie's house—the desk is totally destroyed—the ivory collection...."

"I'll be right there."

"Right there" was nearly immediately. I was on the deck separating pieces of ivory from shards of glass when David arrived with chamomile teas and vanilla lattes. Two of each.

"I didn't know which way you were going: fuel up or calm down," he stated, extending the calm-down cup of chamomile a snitch closer to me than the latte.

"Nice try," I said, taking the latte, and a peek at his face. That eye-twinkle and lopsided grin gets me every time. "Oh, and thanks," I blubbered.

Although it took us close to an hour to put the house back in some semblance of order, I was satisfied that Jackie would be spared the worst of it. Chloe and Jackie had probably finished their bike ride and were waiting for me at Fog Island. David accepted my invitation to breakfast, and on our drive into town, talked me through my anger to the gentlest way of breaking the news to Jackie.

We found Chloe and Jackie waiting on the bench in front of the popular cafe surrounded by a group of less patient breakfast seekers. My sisters had finished their ride about fifteen minutes ago and had checked in with Greg, the cafe host and a former student of mine. Our name was next on the list.

"How ya doing, Ms. Marshall?" inquired Greg.

He's nearly forty, has three kids of his own, and still calls me Ms. Marshall. I have given up trying to get him to call me Maggie, and no longer bother with my sarcastic, "Fine, thank you, *Mr.* Anderson."

Knowing how to yield is strength. I had read that just this morning in the *Tao Te Ch'ing*. Every morning I read a passage from the short, wisdom-loaded book, and have probably read that passage hundreds of times. I'm slowly learning what it means in my life.

Yielding is the way of the Tao. I have yielded. Greg will probably call me Ms. Marshall for another 105 years.

As Greg ushered us to a table, he gave us a quick update on the kids, a progress report on his master's thesis, and showed us a picture of the new commercial fishing boat he hoped to buy. We small-talked our way through the seating and confirmed that we would be going to Landmark House on Thursday to visit with his ailing dad.

During all the diversionary chatter, my anger at Boston and nagging worries for Jackie were mounting. I needed to get a grip. As if he could follow the course of my struggle, David filled the space with more small talk and menu passing, giving me time to reassemble the composure I would need to tell Jackie what awaited her at home.

"I'm afraid the desk and chair may be beyond repair, but a few of the ivory pieces are intact," I concluded.

"Maybe some others can be mended. David already called Caleb to fix the window; he's probably there now."

Jackie's expected explosion never came. Just total, defeated acceptance. Gentle Chloe was the one who reacted. She was ready to march across the street to the police station, swear out a warrant, and send Boston to San Quentin for a couple of eternities.

"Are you sure you want to read about this in the paper on Thursday?" David asked her. "Wouldn't that be the second time this month Jackie's name has been in the Police Blotter section?"

"Third," I added. "That's why I didn't call the cops right away. I figured that was Jackie's decision."

Chloe sat back down.

"Let's eat," said Jackie, lifting her chin. Her eyes were steely, her jaw was set. I could tell she was wound as tight as a compressed spring. Boston wasn't out of her crosshairs, but for the moment, he was out of the conversation.

Over the best *huevos rancheros* on the island, Chloe and I filled David in on the latest developments in our mystery. "So, of course, the $64,000 question is why would Boston have a phosphorous container?" mused David. "And did he receive $1,000 from that fellow in the bar? If so, why?"

"And is there a connection between the Scowlies, Frick and Frack, and Boston? And, does it have something to do with the hush-hush meeting that could be taking place right now, next door to Aunt Amy's?"

As if it had heard her name, my phone jingled with Aunt Amy's ringtone: "Nineteenth Nervous Breakdown."

"Thorazine. Come get me," she ordered. "I finally have proof. Sherburne is lacing our food with Thorazine."

Oh, for crying out loud.

"Knew it all along; now I have the proof. Come get me before it gets cold."

"I gotta get Aunt Amy before her evidence cools." Even Jackie couldn't help but laugh as I explained the latest get-out-of-Sherburne ploy.

"I'll drive you," offered David, taking my elbow and grabbing the entire tab for breakfast. "Who knows?" he laughed. "My chemistry background might come in handy."

"Why don't you drop Aunt Amy at my house after?" suggested Chloe. "I'm setting up the big loom for the Conservation Foundation fundraiser weaving project. Even one-handed, Aunt Amy can warp faster than I can weft."

"Deal."

The bottom of Main Street was chock full of last night's merrymakers. There was comfort in knowing that by this time tomorrow the Figawi folks would have taken their hangovers back to the mainland. However, at the moment most of them were ambling and shuffling across the cobbles, clumping together mid-street to commiserate with cronies, and blocking traffic as effectively as Parisian barricades.

Too polite to sit on the horn, David edged his car gently through the crowds. "And don't holler out the window, Maggie," he warned. "Most of these folks will mosey up to the pharmacy, looking for a little something for their throbbing heads and furry tongues. Money, money, money for me."

As requested by Mr. Chamber of Commerce, I kept my mouth shut. Not one single, "Get out of the damn road" slipped from my lips.

Aunt Amy was waiting in front of Sherburne. Samuel the gardener — probably alerted that she would be there — was nowhere in sight.

When Aunt Amy spots David, she morphs from kooky curmudgeon to saucy soubrette in less than a nanosecond. If it weren't so comically ludicrous, it would be sickening. David finds it far more amusing than the rest of us. In fact, he's been accused of egging her on more than a few times.

"May I?" the ever-courtly David asked, extending his arm and maneuvering her into my just-vacated spot in the front.

"Delighted, I'm sure." I swear she batted her eyes like some pimply-faced teenager.

ACK ATTACK

Gag. To both of them.

"Evidence. Got the evidence, David. I've finally caught them red-handed," she said conspiratorially while clutching a Styrofoam cooler to her chest. "Thorazine. Thorazine in the chipped beef."

I wasn't playing, but sportive David jumped right in and pressed her for details, finally offering to send her purloined samples to his lab for testing. "We'll nail it down cold with hot chipped beef, Mrs. Delano."

Oh, brother.

By the time we got out to Chloe's, Aunt Amy had given David no fewer than eighty-three instructions on securing the proper chain of evidence, and had extracted his promise to photographically document each step. *CSI* had taught her well.

Chloe met us when we pulled up to her house, and graciously collected the ersatz Sherlock. David secured the "evidence" and dropped me home. "See you at the picnic at six o'clock. I'd pick you up, but I've got to work 'til closing. They'll be lined up at the counter all day complaining of headaches, heartburn, and sunburn—expecting a cure-all for self-indulgence, no doubt."

212

A cheery wave, the characteristic smile, and he was on his way back to town "to do his drug dealer thing," as Shad puts it. Wondering if he had deliberately avoided a reference to our upcoming Saturday night "date" or if it had merely slipped his mind, I mused and dawdled my way into the house to check on Shad. Still sleeping. I headed out to the garden.

I might as well have a sign posted in my garden: *Ye Olde Snack Shoppe.* Not that the rabbits and deer need any help recognizing their cafeteria. It seemed they had no trouble last night and had munched their way through my entire lettuce crop. They didn't bother the more aromatic greenery: the cilantro, parsley, and chard. However, there was not a pea left on a vine or a leaf of spinach more than nub-high.

Ah, yes. The way of the Tao. Yield.

I made a mental note to check the Bumf Box tomorrow to see if the organic rabbit repellant had arrived. Bumf comes from "bum fodder," which was nineteenth century British schoolboy slang to associate unwanted printed matter (like tests) with toilet paper. Since "unwanted printed matter" describes most of the mail I receive, Phil—whose job it was as a teen to drive to town and collect the mail from the box at the post office — renamed it the Bumf Box and called his daily mail runs the Fanny Express.

If the rabbit repellant hadn't arrived, I might have to unearth my trusty ole Indian scarecrow. Made one spring as a Mothers' Day gift by Stan and Jack, this nearly-nude statue of a Native American was designed to look like the Indian on the original state seal of Massachusetts. The naked Native on the old Massachusetts seal had a speak bubble coming out of his mouth: "Come over and help us."

I always assumed this plea was nothing more than eighteenth century colonial ethnocentrism. The Wampanoags did not need or want any help from the land-snatching British.

The boys, well schooled in their Massachusetts history and well practiced in puns at my expense, added an original speak bubble to their scarecrow. They cleverly replaced "Come over and help us" with a speak bubble that read, "Come in and help yourself." They still celebrate that scarecrow as one of their top ten pranks.

With absolutely no desire to waste this day rummaging through the musty garage to find my scarecrow, I hoped the vegetable garden was healthy enough to withstand one more night of rabbit foraging. I'd weed the beans and strawberries instead, then take a break and go out to Tom Nevers to collect Shad's forgotten clipboard. My back and knees would thank me for the respite.

With the Figawi race as an enjoyable distraction, I knee-walked down the rows, yanking, plucking, and digging. Satisfied that I had done a fairly honest morning's work, I looked in on Shad and grabbed another cup of coffee for the road trip to Tom Nevers. Maybe Jackie would want to go with me. I drove past Chloe's and made the U-turn up to Jackie's, honking a beep-beep, pause, beep-beep to signal my arrival.

"Well, at least he's gotten all his stuff outta here," said a tremulous Jackie as she approached the truck. She made no further attempt to hide her tear-stained anger as she climbed into the front seat. "I don't care where you're going. I'm going too."

Slam.

"Did you *see* my car? Did you *see* it? The driver's side of my car?"

Uh-oh.

215

"My favorite bumper sticker? War Doesn't Decide Who's Right, Only Who's Left? Now it says, War Does Right! He's totally caved in the whole side of my car! Look!"

So he had, and so it did: War Does Right.

"We can cover it with duct tape," I offered.

My half-baked solution provoked a growl. Playing the Mom card didn't help much either. "Remember what Mom always said: it's the hurt people who hurt people."

"*Hurt*?" she screeched incredulously. "*Hurt*? *I* am crushed. I'm dangerous. And don't try to put any of that forgiveness crap on me."

Okey dokey.

I chitter-chattered mindlessly the rest of the way to the rotary in a futile attempt to divert her from her ferocious misery. Nope. How about the radio? Music, after all, is supposed to soothe the savage beast.

It is hard to stay mad when the radio is playing twangy country, the sky is a crystal clear blue, and the clouds look like a kindergartener's rendition of sky. Jackie's edges had softened by the time we reached the entrance to the fields, and she was joining me in a lusty sing-along to Johnny Cash's "Ring of Fire."

Midway through the chorus, "down, down, down, and the flames went higher," we pulled onto the perimeter road by the fields and nearly met our Maker. A screech of brakes and an abrupt swerve were all that kept us from a head-on collision with the car careening wildly around the corner.

Jackie cursed; I screamed. The gray car accelerated.

The gray car with the three guys in it.

The nondescript gray car with the three Scowly-faced guys in it.

In a huge hurry.

CHAPTER 14 – A Dirty Lab

"Damn, that was close! They were going a zillion miles an hour!" yelped Jackie. "They almost killed us!"

"Did you *see* who was in the car? Did you *see*? The Three Scowlies!"

I pulled over to catch my breath and collect my racing thoughts.

Jackie said it first. "Hey, let's go see if we can figure out what they were doing."

Although I was not 100 percent sure I wanted to sleuth about, I was not going to let Jackie do it alone. "I bet it has something to do with that abandoned bunker. Let's start there," I suggested with transparent false bravado.

Sure enough. Although someone had made a half-hearted attempt to restore the Keep Out sign and to replace the boards across the door, it was apparent that the entrance had been tampered with. A few missing nails and the misaligned lumber made the replacement boarding look hurried and careless.

"So, are we going inside?" I asked semi-rhetorically. There was always the remote chance that Jackie would try to talk us out of it.

Since she was already busy trying to wrench open the door, I guessed the answer was yes. The breaking and entering part proved to be simple. The replacement boarding had been as haphazard as it had appeared, and the boards came loose with a few determined yanks.

"I don't suppose you have another flashlight in that Everything Bag of yours?" I gulped.

"Yup, but it's home. Come on. Last one inside is a tofu burger."

I happen to like tofu burgers. I don't happen to like windowless, dank, dark, cave-like spaces that have probably just been visited by three sinister men. I went in anyway — as the tofu burger. Jackie went in first.

"Yuck. Cobwebs," I whimpered, brushing a few stray, sticky wisps out of my face.

Crash. Stumble. "Ouch! Damn it!"

"Jackie, are you OK? Jackie? Where *are* you?"

"Fine, fine. Over here. Just a barked shin. But I might have found a lamp or something." She had. It appeared to be some sort of oil lamp with a wick. No matches, though.

"If you promise not to ask me why I'm carrying matches, I'll take them out of my pocket," she said. "And you can't ask me later either. Off limits."

"Yup. OK." I guess Jackie hadn't been as successful kicking her smoking habit as she would have liked us to believe. At the moment, I wasn't about to quibble.

I have never been in a real chemistry lab. The lab at school, however, looks enough like what I was seeing here to tell me that this bunker had very recently been used as a makeshift lab. Discarded beakers, a scale, and a bunch of curly glass tubing glinted in the lamp light. Rubber gloves—lots of them—and some had a sort of melted look.

And containers. Phosphorous containers.

The dots were connecting. The Scowlies to phosphorous; Phosphorous to Boston; Boston to the Scowlies and to whatever was in the envelope. But how did Frick and Frack connect? Was there a connection to Senator Marques's secret meeting? And just *what* were they making in here? *Oooo*, and what if they were coming back to check on it?

"Let's get outta here. This place is making my skin crawl." This from the intrepid Jackie just as I was about to suggest the very same thing.

Only too happy to lead the way *out*, I emerged into the glare of the noonday sun, squinting and brushing off a few real, but mostly imagined, spider webs and crawly things.

"I think we gotta go back in; try to take some pictures with your phone," Jackie said bravely.

"Here's my phone. You go."

Jackie wasn't having any of that. I swallowed my jitters and followed her in. The pictures were blurry,

222

the lab equipment indistinct, but it was the best we could do. "Now, to the cops," said Jackie, the newly self-appointed chief of this adventure.

Eager to leave the dismal interior, I zipped outside before Jackie could change her mind. "And just what in the world are we gonna say to the cops that doesn't sound like we have lost our feeble minds?" I countered. "Let's see: 'Officer, we have uncovered a secret lab used by three Scowly-faced bad guys who are going to do something really dreadful. We don't know what, but they're using phosphorous that has been made into...well, we don't know that either. And we think they're probably going to do it to Senator Marques, and whoever is at his house, for whatever secret meeting is going on there.'"

"They'll measure us for straitjackets," Jackie conceded.

"Get in the truck. Just get in the truck. Let's go. We'll figure out something on the way home." I had no idea what we would figure out, but I sure didn't want to stick around in case our scowly-faced scientists were planning to return.

"Don't forget Shad's clipboard," reminded Jackie.

Oops.

The clipboard was just where she had said it would be, but a great deal soggier than when she had left it. The fog had settled comfortably into the paper, and most of her rosters and game plays were now a single, sodden, wavy mass of pulp. Nantucketized.

Hoping Shad would be able to salvage something useful from the damp blob on the clipboard, I tossed it on the backseat, backed the truck around, and jounced out to the pot-holed road.

"I don't think we should call the cops yet," I temporized. "Let's get a think tank together. We'll go to my house, wake Shad, and call Chloe and Brett. David's working, so he's out, but the rest of us ought to be able to make some sense of this."

Only too happy to ratchet it down a bit, Jackie agreed. In her typical ADHD way, she commenced with sharing her grandson Connick's Memorial Day feats. The four-week-old prodigy had managed a perfectly timed, full-shouldered shrug and bored yawn—right in the middle of his dad's complaints about his every-two-hour feeding demands. Jackie had the video to prove it. She'd already forwarded

224

it to my phone, and to every other phone of every other person she knew on the entire East Coast.

The bike path along the side of Milestone Road looked like rush hour in New York City. Bikes, strollers, runners, walkers—everyone was hurrying along to keep their heart rates in some prescribed cardio zone. No one even noticed the herd of wildebeest and the zebra on the Serengeti across the street.

Every year some unknown islander makes new wooden cutouts of African animals and places them out on the heathland near Tom Nevers. Sections of our moors look very much like the Serengeti plains where real African beasties roam and roar, and the similarities must be simply too compelling for some clever artist. Every year he (she?) puts up new animals, and every year the town takes them down.

Last year we had a couple of lions and a giraffe. This year it was wildebeests and a zebra. I often wished I knew who our secret Serengeti Trespasser was—not so I could tell anyone else; just so I could send a secret thank you.

Many tourists leave the island with T-shirts embossed with I Am the Man from Nantucket. The

Serengeti Animal Maker, in my mind, *is* the Man from Nantucket. That playful spirit of mischief, the tenacity, the bold creativity, the nose-thumbing independence, and the chutzpah—that is more Nantucket to me than some man who knows some woman with a body part "bigger than a bucket."

The most popular tourist T-shirt—the Man from Nantucket one—comes in many colors, and they were all well represented along the bike path. Another popular tourist tee, I Live on Nantucket in the Gray-shingled House with the White Trim, is available in only one color—gray—with plain white lettering. Artistic gestalt, I suppose. Although not *all* houses on Nantucket are gray with white trim, most of them seem to be, and all three Marshall sisters are in banal compliance with the T-shirt.

Our island's 45 mph super highway—Milestone Road—got us to the rotary in a jiffy, and there we stayed. Although it didn't seem possible that people could need any more groceries, the waiting line to get into Stop and Shop's parking lot had spilled out onto Sparks Avenue, backed up traffic to the rotary, and generated some short-tempered horn honking. Knowing that snaggled traffic is the way of summer, I refrained from letting my impatience increase the din.

We crept past Stop and Shop and were immediately stalled again. The high school is on the left, just past the grocery store, and across the street from that is the Boys & Girls Club. Although the busy, four-way intersection there flaunts one of the most elegant ancient elm trees on the island, it also fosters year-round traffic jams. In the summer, these jam-ups are a legendary nuisance.

It took us a good ten minutes to inch our way the hundred yards to the intersection and to turn — finally — onto Prospect Street. Thank goodness the traffic thinned, and it was a clear run home after that. Even my impatience was impatient, and I was in no mood for any more traffic snags.

Beep! Beep! Pause. Beep! Beep!

Brett waved as we passed his house and Jackie hollered out the window. "Get Chloe! Come down to Maggie's!" The edgy note of urgency in her voice was enough to get Brett's attention. He abandoned his lawn mower tinkering and went to get Chloe.

Once inside, I went to the kitchen to put on a pot of fresh coffee, and Jackie went to wake up Shad. I could hear the gentle murmurings of my sleepy daughter as she and Jackie girl-talked and giggled.

Jackie's earlier rage clearly had dissipated, and with luck, may have fizzled out altogether. Her blood pressure can't stand too much of that high-intensity fury. Neither can mine.

"*Whoo-hoo!*" Chloe. Announcing their arrival.

"Where's Aunt Amy?" I asked, expecting her to waltz in behind them.

"Out like a light." Chloe grinned. "One of Brett's high-test Bloody Marys."

"Self-defense," said Brett sheepishly.

A yawning Shad got the coffee while I filled them in on what we had found out at Tom Nevers. As I veered off into speculation about what I thought the presence of a lab and phosphorous might mean, Brett called a halt.

"Wait. It seems to me that if we can't figure out *what* they were making out there, then we don't have a snowball's chance in hell of convincing anyone to take this seriously. We don't know who they are, what they were doing, why, or how."

Unfortunately, we all had to agree that he was right.

Shad, the woman of action, fired up the computer. A well-practiced Googler, she followed links to all sorts of phosphorous-related subjects: fertilizers, cap gun ammunition, incendiary bombs, and sarin. She kept coming back to sarin.

Sarin? Like the gas used in Japan in the 1995 subway attack by those terrorists? No one wanted sarin gas to be a dot that was in any way connected to any one of our puzzle pieces.

Brett, reading over Shad's shoulder, brought us back from the brink. "It says here that sarin gas is highly toxic. If it isn't handled extremely carefully, it's lethal. These three guys seem more like the Three Stooges than the Three Sinister Scowlies. I mean, really, that sarin stuff is for honest-to-God terrorists. These guys sound like buffoons."

Although I wasn't totally convinced that they were buffoons, I couldn't offer much evidence to the contrary. They had, in fact, been amateurishly bumbling about.

Jackie and Chloe were quick to agree with Brett. "Even if they were capable of making sarin," added Jackie, "this article makes it quite clear that delivering the gas is the hardest part. I don't think these guys are up to it. They couldn't even nail up a bunch of boards properly. Right?"

"Right," supported Chloe. "They couldn't even pass an envelope without being seen."

"Yes, but—"

"On the other hand—"

"However—"

We were spinning our collective mental wheels in circles.

Brett had had enough. "We've been over and over this, eight ways to Sunday. The dots don't connect. Let's give it a rest."

"But wait a minute," said Jackie. "How does Boston fit in this picture?"

Shad fielded that one. "Well, we know that he was handed an envelope at Cy's *and* that he fled the scene when he realized that you guys had seen him. We also know he had a phosphorous container in his stuff. Other than that, we've got nothing. It's all circumstantial. Guesswork."

"Circumstantial or not, *I* think the envelope had the $1,000 in it," I said. "I also think that the money was from Frick or Frack, or both of them."

"You're on thin ice again, Maggie," said Brett. "Why would Frick or Frack need to pay Boston $1,000?"

"Drugs, probably," grumbled Jackie.

That was the first inkling that Jackie suspected Boston had been farming pot and selling drugs all along. "Best case scenario, they owed him the money for some electrical work, but that seems a bit far-fetched—even to me," she admitted.

Brrring. Brrring.

"Hush! It's Chelsea!" Chloe had whipped her phone out of Brett's back pocket and was frantically pressing buttons.

It was Brett who finally managed to answer the phone. "What? Chelsea? Hello? Is that you? Is the baby—?"

It was Trevor, Chelsea's husband, calling from the delivery room. The trampoline had worked.

"We'll be right there."

Right there? The delivery room was about 250 miles away.

All thoughts of Boston, sarin, and the Scowlies were forgotten. Chloe took off for home to pack, while Brett stayed with the phone to make the travel arrangements.

Chloe was successful. Brett was not. The mass Figawi exodus and the stranded passengers grounded by last night's fog had claimed all available seats on every single flight and on every single boat for the rest of the day. There was nothing available but standby until the next morning.

If you're an off-islander, this might be a travel nightmare. For Nantucketers, it's travel as usual. Many similar nightmares have taught us that it is better to be philosophically patient rather than frustrated and annoyed.

Brett got seats on the six thirty flight the next morning and crossed his fingers that Maushop would keep his smoky fog to himself. Just in case the airport was fogged in, Brett booked two tickets on the seven fifteen boat as well. The proud grandparents-to-be would be in New Jersey by early afternoon, one way or another.

Shad had abandoned the computer and was rummaging in the freezer for the hot dogs for tonight's picnic. "Ma! Did you know you still have the carcass from last year's Thanksgiving turkey in here? And something that looks like a frozen Chia Pet."

"Turkey noodle soup," I replied. "Not sure about the green stuff." Cooking is not high on my list of priorities. It's not low on the list either. It's simply not on the list at all. "Speaking of the unidentifiable, wait 'til you see the papers on your clipboard."

"Nantucketized?" She wasn't expecting an answer.

Shad found the hot dogs as well as some frostbitten buns. I'd have to add some of my hoarded gourmet olives to our picnic fare. I even had a few dozen chocolate chip cookies and snickerdoodles stashed away for just such emergencies.

We also found enough odds and ends for some lunch. Shad put out a tray of cold cuts, sliced cheeses, and homemade pickles. Brett found a half loaf of Portuguese bread and some sesame bagels. I discovered a patch in the garden that the rabbits had missed and added a bowl of arugula, chervil, spinach, and borage. With mayo, mustard, and horseradish (for Brett), we were all set.

"Lunch. Come and get it," I announced.

As if on cue, Aunt Amy tottered in. "Baby! The baby's coming. Where's Brett? He's got to be told."

"He knows," we all chorused.

Our lunch talk was as light as the meal: "Was it a boy or girl?", "Have they decided on the name?", "Was Chelsea still planning to make it through labor without drugs?", "How will Trevor manage to keep his pushy mother out of the delivery room?"

Afterward, we all scattered to scavenge in garages for beach gear, gather our stashed-away picnic supplies, and load our vehicles. Shad agreed to drive Aunt Amy out to Sherburne as she was insisting that she had to go get wine, some pate, and a jacket. I correctly suspected that she was also hoping to score some more evidence.

"Onion dip. They've got Thorazine in the onion dip too, I bet. Every afternoon when they put out the tea sandwiches? Well, they put out chips and dip

234

too. Ellery Macomber eats that dip all the time—can't remember her own name."

Aunt Amy described the details of her latest suspicions to Shad in admirable cloak and dagger fashion as they headed out the back door. "That dip's always tasted a little bit off to me. I was telling Jane Jorgensen just the other day...."

I made quick work of the paper towel lunch dishes and headed back to the gardens. Each year in the early spring, I realize that my gardens have gotten impossibly far ahead of me. The weeds are out of control, and I am out of youthful vigor. I'll never be able to catch up. Not too many years ago, I could manage a ten-hour day of weeding, hauling, and hoeing. Maybe half of that these days. As I have learned to accept the limitations of my aging, I have also learned to accept the lessons of my garden:

Enough: Know when enough is the best you can do.

Control: Learn to accept and even enjoy that which you cannot control.

Perfection: It will never be, so let it be.

Gratitude: Look at the flowers, not the weeds.

Patience: If you force it, you'll lose it.

Simplicity: Less can be more.

The gentle afternoon passed quickly. Shad and Aunt Amy — evidence bagged and tagged in plastic — returned with the wine and pate, as well as a rhubarb pie from a bake sale at the Salt Marsh Senior Center. Chloe called — no baby yet. They would meet us at Hulbert. Jackie called — could she ride with us?

Forced to forage in the garage after all, I unearthed the abandoned picnic gear. After de-molding the cooler and adding another layer of duct tape to the wind-tattered beach umbrella, I gathered the food, a thermos of lemon mint iced tea, and stowed it all in the back of the truck.

Aunt Amy and Shad, along with the pate, wine, and rapidly disappearing cookies, were in the backseat. Jackie rode shotgun. The radio was wailing country music, and even Aunt Amy joined in our off-key, tone-deaf rendition of "Coal Miner's Daughter."

Midway through the final chorus, we turned onto Hulbert Avenue.

Son of a gun. What was that just pulling out of Hulbert?

A gray car.

A nondescript gray car.

A nondescript gray car with three Scowly-faced passengers — followed by a familiar, rusted, wreck of a truck with Boston behind the wheel.

CHAPTER 15 — The Picnic

I hung a U-ey. No more shilly-shallying. I was going to find out what was going on.

"Stop that car!" ordered Aunt Amy. "Stop it!"

"The *car*? What about Boston's truck?" I challenged.

Boston had continued around the rotary. The gray car raced in the opposite direction, down Easton Street.

"No, no, not Boston. The gray car," she commanded.

"Follow the gray car. They're getting away. Hurry!"

"Trying!" I sighed with exasperation.

"Sneakers. I caught those sneaky Petes two weeks ago," Aunt Amy explained. "Skulking about the grounds like a bunch of thieves. They ran for it.

239

Took off just when I was reading them their rights. Wish I'd had my gun."

Hoping she didn't have it with her now, I kept up my quixotic pursuit of the fleeing car. Nantucket's narrow, one-way streets do not lend themselves to Hollywood style, high-speed chases. Neither does a clumsy, lumbering vehicle like a pickup truck.

We lost them somewhere between Children's Beach and the Whaling Museum. There was no sense in going after Boston's truck; it would be long gone as well. Ignoring Aunt Amy's critique of my driving prowess ("lackluster, inept, and ham-fisted"), I turned back to Easton and headed toward Hulbert. I was anxious to see what Brett would make of this latest "coincidence."

It looked like the same black SUVs were still hogging the parking spaces near Aunt Amy's. A bit resentfully, I offloaded Shad, Aunt Amy, and the gear in front of the gate, parked down on Walsh Street, and trooped back in time to hear my aunt broadcasting her opinion of Ernie Whitehead to the entire neighborhood.

"Cockalorum. Just an old cockalorum. A boasting braggart." Shad's ineffectual attempts to lower

240

DENNIE DORAN

Aunt Amy's volume were met with, "And I don't care who hears me," shouted in the general direction of Ernie's house.

"Give it a rest. His car's not in his driveway. He's not even home," I said testily.

"Justine can hear me. She'll make sure he knows. Hope that nosey snitch is calling him right now," argued the old pot stirrer.

We gathered up our picnic paraphernalia, and without thinking, took the usual route to the beach—straight through Aunt Amy's front gate.

"Halt!"

Yikes.

I have never been on the target end of a weapon. It was Frack (or Frick?) on the business end. "Sorry. Sorry. We were only—"

"Special Agent Chester? If I may?" Mike Gaspee, a former classmate and currently a sergeant with the Nantucket Police Department was with him. "Special Agent Chester, this is Mrs. Delano. As you know, this is her house. Can't we just let these good folks pass through? Looks like they're just going to the beach for a picnic. No harm in that, eh?"

Mike's appeal appeased Special Agent Chester, but not his tough-nut partner. We weren't out of the soup and might have stayed there had it not been for the serendipitous arrival of Ernie Whitehead. Ernie's arrivals are not usually considered serendipitous. In fact, his arrivals are usually considered a stroke of ill luck or rotten timing. Possibly both. This time, however, it was quite the opposite.

Apparently, Ernie had been successfully brown-nosing the Feds. It would seem that his rabid Republican proclivities did not prevent him from schmoozing with "socialist-loving Democrats." He was probably trying to promote the use of *his* house for the Secret Service. Contrary to what Ernie had said yesterday, an official presidential appreciation at the White House, even from "a pinko liberal," must have been worth courting.

I was not sure how Ernie had convinced the Secret Service that he was a man of any importance at all. Most who know him peg him for the pompous windbag he is. Meddlesome and self-righteous as well. Nonetheless, I was grateful that the surprisingly gullible Frick and Frack seemed taken in by his charade.

"Surely, Officer Chester—*ahem*—surely a dowager is entitled to visit her kingdom without rebuke," intoned Ernie.

Dowager? Kingdom?

Who in their right mind would listen to someone who spoke as if he were trying out for a part in a kindergarten *Camelot* play?

Frick and Frack, or so it seemed. After conferring briefly in whispers, they ordered Mike to escort us down Aunt Amy's path, help us collect her grill from the porch, and see that we had settled ourselves on the beach in front of her house.

Odd too, for the first time in decades, Aunt Amy had managed to keep her mouth shut. No verbal sparring with Ernie, no haughty scoldings, no threats or challenges. Nothing.

When I was certain that our beach access had been assured, I risked giving her a two-fingered V for victory and a har-dee-har elbow to the side. Still no response. Rather, she looked like she might be rolling golf balls around in her mouth. Undulating bumps and lumps made their way across her cheeks. With a muttered *"Fumfck"* and a stamp of her right foot, she spat the nomadic golf balls into her hands. Dentures.

As she worked her upper left bridge back into place, I silently thanked it for choosing just the right time to come loose. Any Aunt Amy participation in the previous conversation could have sent all of us on a one-way trip to Guantanamo, leaving the obsequious Ernie behind to gloat, toady, and besmirch our names.

As we rounded the corner by the front porch, I could see Brett and Chloe conferring down by the water's edge. Josh was setting up the tables; Grace, his girlfriend, was sorting through the chairs. Shad was somewhere behind us lugging the cooler, unimpeded (I hoped) by Ernie-the-sycophant or the officious authorities.

After exchanging hurried hugs and how-are-you's with Josh and Grace, Aunt Amy and I headed straight for Brett. What, I wondered, would he make of this latest "coincidence"?

Preoccupied with the baby's imminent arrival, Brett was not very interested in any coincidences at all. As we tried repeatedly to draw his attention to the possible significance of our newest development, he tried equally as hard to ignore it. Constantly responding to text messages from Trevor or talking to Chloe with foreheads together, Brett only responded with a half-hearted, "Interesting, interesting." Shifty Boston and little nondescript cars did not really interest him at all. Aunt Amy's exaggeratedly vivid account of her aborted citizen's arrest last week didn't do much for our credibility either.

We gave up. Even *we* were finding ourselves tiresome.

"Ma, come sit down," said Shad. "And here, put on some sunscreen. Did you bring your sweatshirt? It's going to cool off."

Who was the mom here, anyway?

Shad had done the lion's share of the hauling and had plopped herself and her Cisco Gray Lady beer into a faded canvas beach chair. The nearly empty cookie bag was on her lap.

"Chair? Where's my favorite chair?"

I could see Aunt Amy's favorite chair. Looking more like scrap iron, the rusted relic had been stashed in a heap back toward the house.

"It's too rusty to be safe, Aunt Amy," soothed Josh, pointing to a brand new, low slung, ground-hugging chair. "Try this one."

"Never. I'm not getting in, and I couldn't get out."

Raising and lowering his eyebrows Groucho-style and curling an imaginary Errol Flynn mustache, Josh scooped Aunt Amy in his arms and swoop-plopped her into the chair. "Wait 'til you see how I get you out. Practically X-rated."

The old dear actually blushed.

"It's a girl! It's a girl!" Chloe, arms waving madly, was outracing Brett up from the water's edge. "It's a girl! A girl!"

"Eight pounds and four ounces. Another redhead," she panted. "They're naming her Maeve."

Jackie had thought to bring champagne. We boisterously welcomed Maeve to the family, toasted the new parents and grandparents, the great grandmother, the great aunts, and the cousins. By the second bottle of champagne, we had sent calls and text messages through the entire family phone tree.

"We'd better eat before we start on that third bottle," advised Shad.

As with all our potluck events, the most amazing variety of food appeared in an instant. Our proletariat hot dogs and beans joined deviled eggs, pot stickers, brie puffs, and smoked salmon. Since no one had thought to bring plates, we were preparing to use the lids from the plastic storage containers as substitutes.

No need. With a hail of hounds, Cousin Elizabeth arrived pulling three giant picnic hampers, two diaper bags, one of her daughter Carolyn's triplets, and a cooler, all on a huge toboggan. Carolyn followed with a second toboggan loaded with yet another cooler, two Trader Joe bags filled to the brim, and the other two of the triplets. Of course, *Cousin Elizabeth* and *Carolyn* had remembered plates—and linen napkins. Even a corkscrew and ketchup. Always a good idea to include at least one Type A on a picnic's guest list.

"Gam! Gam!" The first triplet jumped on Aunt Amy's lap. Triplets two and three piled on top. Butch and

Clyde were next. Aunt Amy might have weathered the enthusiastic welcome unscathed had it not been for Bonnie and Sundance. The tipping point came when Triplet Number Two pushed Triplet Number One into Sundance. Sundance yelped and lurched, launching Bonnie's hind end into Triplet Number Three just a he was leaning in for a good *whomp* at the back of Triplet Number One's head.

The whole house of cards tipped. Then toppled.

Ass-over-tea-kettle, sky-pointing legs scissoring the air, Aunt Amy's "*Jssssshhh! Jsssssshhhh!*" was taken to mean that she was calling Josh in for the rescue.

As promised, his strategy to get her out of her chair was outrageous. Straddling his grandmother, Josh engulfed her in a giant bear hug, half lifted and half swung her upright, and then whirled her free of the melee. Triplet Number Three earned a glancing blow to the head from Aunt Amy's left Ked, a fitting consequence for the attack on his brother that had started the tipping and toppling.

"Carolyn, get what's-his-name off of Clyde. Bonnie, come here. Heel. *Heel!*" Cousin Elizabeth

248

commanded ineffectively, yet again. "Oh, someone grab Butch before he—"

Too late. Triplets Number One and Two were pinned.

Click. Click. Click.

Ernie Whitehead, with a camera, recording the brawling scuffle. "For my slide show at the next Neighborhood Association meeting. You're all invited, of course."

"Bugger off, Ernie." Guess Aunt Amy's dentures were still in place despite her tumble.

Ernie, hastily back tracking, click-clicked himself down the beach. He had probably gathered enough evidence to have the dogs euthanized. Maybe my aunt, too.

"Come on, dogs. Let's go for a swim." Josh to the rescue again.

As he and Grace rounded up the beagles, Jackie and Cousin Elizabeth got Aunt Amy steadied on her pins. Her pockets and scalp were loaded with sand and the side of her sweater was coated in dog drool. Other than that, no harm had been done.

Carolyn lured the little Huns down the beach with promises to help them build a giant sand castle.

"Ma! I forgot to tell you about the scammers," blurted Shad. "They hit up bars in Provincetown, Wellfleet, and Chatham just last week. By sheer luck, the officer on duty at the police station had just read a fax about them from the sheriff's office."

"Scammers? What scammers?" Aunt Amy hadn't heard about Ascot and Stiletto. As we filled her in, Brett shared the pictures of Chelsea and Maeve that Trevor had just texted. Trevor also informed the besotted grandfather that Maeve was twenty-four inches long, could bellow like an auctioneer, and had Coatue for a middle name.

Coatue is a fragile barrier beach separating the harbor from Nantucket Sound. Its rolling sand dunes, delicate maritime flora, salt marshes, and tidal ponds are a refuge for shorebirds, horseshoe crabs, and solitude-seeking islanders. It is as close to seventh heaven as one might hope to get.

It is not, however, much of a middle name.

Maeve Coatue Brady?

I thought I understood what may have prompted Chelsea to tag her daughter with such a middle name. Like all Marshalls, I love Coatue and have spent many hours, weekends, and even weeks at our shack out there. There is something magically restorative about being in a tiny, tiny shack with no electricity, running water, or amenities. Just you and nature, like Thoreau at Walden. Only better, even more simplified and remote.

Sometimes we would go out in a family herd. Sometimes one of us goes out just to be alone. Out the Wauwinet Road, stop at the Gatehouse, let some air out of the tires, and then just drive over miles of sand, or cross the harbor by boat. Either way, once you are there, you are embraced by the primal simplicity of nature. There is no experience quite like it.

There have also been any number of comic episodes out there, usually involving a guest one of us has brought out to the shack. There was Chloe's friend who used poison ivy rather than bayberry to wipe her bum; Jackie's date who wallowed and hollered unnoticed in the Sound for a good twenty minutes after toppling unseen off the back of her Sunfish; and, the memorable Lock Out.

My son Phil had brought a date to one of our Coatue family weeks. For many reasons, none of which were apparent to the dewy-eyed Phil, we all disliked her. She treated Phil like a moron, expected me to wait on her, and flatly refused to help out with any chores. On the fifth day of our week-long retreat, Jack, Shad, and The Dragon Lady drove out to Great Point Lighthouse to meet up with Phil and Chelsea, who were fishing for blues. Halfway there, Alison—aka The Dragon Lady—had to make a pit stop. Nature had called.

Off she went seeking some shrub tall enough to protect her modesty. In a flash, she was racing frantically back to the truck. Mosquitoes. Swarms of voracious, determined mosquitoes clouded all around her.

Although to this day neither Jack nor Shad will point the finger, *one* of them locked the truck doors. *Both* of them pretended that the locks were jammed and feigned frantic unlocking motions while Alison, beating madly on the windows and slapping ineffectively at the buzzing carnivores, was devoured.

In a minute (or two) Jack and Shad had "fixed" the problem and unlocked the doors. Within the hour,

Alison was nearly unrecognizable: face puffed up and swollen, fingers and toes sausage-like, and red welts all over her arms and legs.

Phil played nursemaid to the whining, poor-me drama queen the rest of the weekend. After that week, we never saw her again. I always wondered if the breakup was Phil's doing or hers.

Well, Maeve Coatue Brady it was. With a third bottle of champagne, we toasted her middle name, sang her a Happy Birthday chorus, and offered hilarious predictions about what kind of parents Chelsea and Trevor would turn out to be.

Brett fired up the grill, I set out the hot dogs, and Chloe dug her baked beans out of the thermal wrap. As Cousin Elizabeth, Carolyn, and the triplets ambled back to the picnic site, we busied ourselves with the feast preparations.

Cousin Elizabeth had outdone herself with an entire smoked ham, caviar with lemon curd, and fresh-baked bread. Carolyn's picnic hamper yielded curried chicken salad and Bartlett's tomatoes with fresh mozzarella and basil. A feast worthy of Henry VIII.

ACK ATTACK

The dogs agreed. Piranha-like, they were all over the food in a flash. Butch took off with the ham as Bonnie grabbed the chicken salad. A bit slower to react, Clyde was stuck with the barely thawed hot dogs. We, the just-robbed diners, flew into action: Josh and Grace took off after the ham; Shad, Brett, and Chloe raced after Clyde and our hot dogs; and Jackie tried to save the chicken salad.

"I'll get it," trilled Aunt Amy, trundling off to help Jackie.

Taking advantage of the pandemonium, I slid off toward her house. Perhaps if I took an oh-so-innocent stroll around Aunt Amy's, I wouldn't arouse the suspicions of the Secret Service at Senator Marques's house. Perhaps I could also find out something that would connect Boston to the Three Scowlies and the senator.

My aunt's house is actually only half a house. The other half of it sits thirty yards away. When Aunt Amy and Uncle Charlie originally purchased the property, there was an enormous, Victorian-era beach "cottage" square in the middle of it. With a hand saw — a *hand saw!* — and his own collection of antique tools, Uncle Charlie cut the dwelling in half, separated the pieces, and created the two spacious houses. Each summer they rented one and lived in the other.

254

I sauntered my way between the two houses, hoping to look like I was simply checking on the gardens. I ineptly mimed a landscaper examining mulch and soil composition while noting plants that may not have fared well over the winter. Ho-humming my way around back, I cut through the fenced-in laundry yard, and slipped through the gate on the senator's side of the property.

Not much to see. I was looking at the utilitarian side of his house. A propane gas tank, the electric meters, two heating units, a dehumidifier, and a huge air conditioner sat on a concrete pad.

So did Boston's tool belt—at least I thought it was his. Hadn't I just stashed it in Jackie's laundry room last night? Yes, I knew it was his. There was the brick red paint on the buckle. Why was it on the concrete pad by Senator Marques's house?

I should have reminded myself that curiosity killed the cat before I tiptoed over there to take a look.

The last thing I remember is bending down to grab the tool belt and hearing a low whistling sound, which must have been followed by a powerful, knockout blow to the back of my head.

CHAPTER 16 — The Cellar

The back of my head was pulsing rhythmically, insistently reminding me that someone had just cracked it a good one. Even after forcing my eyes open, I wasn't sure if I was actually awake. What I could manage to see in the diffused light was overcast with a blurry look and tinged a chemical shade of yellowish green. Forty winks seemed like a mighty fine option — just the remedy for a skull-thumping.

A quick mental scan of all major body parts assured me that I was truly and painfully awake. Wooly-headed, but seeing clearly enough to know that I was in a cellar — Aunt Amy's cellar. I recognized Uncle Charlie's workbench, and there on the wooden wall behind it were his tools, many of which he had made himself. Each tool had its own place, and each place was carefully outlined with white paint to trace the exact shape of the tool that belonged in that exact spot.

257

If you borrowed one of Uncle Charlie's tools, you had best put it back exactly where it had been. Woe betide the child or neighbor who failed to comply. Uncle Charlie could convey a more effective message with a single glance than all the cuss words in the dictionary. No one wanted to be on the receiving end of such a look. The glance that said it all: the dreaded, "I'm not mad at you, just disappointed in you" message. You might have misplaced a tool once. You never did again.

Uncle Charlie had also made himself a unique workbench. Using well-worn oak planks for the top, he had added rows of miniature cabinets for nails and screws to the sides of it and dozens of carefully dovetailed drawers for hinges, braces, and clamps underneath. Uncle Charlie had also hand-lathed hefty blocks of honey-toned oak into sturdy legs to support his workspace. Each of the four well-tooled legs was different: a Morris column, a Doric column, and two types of Essex columns. At the moment, my duct-taped wrists were tied to the fluted Essex one nearest the shoulder vise.

A mottled gray length of old clothesline secured my wrists to the workbench just above the square bun feet Uncle Charlie had added for extra stability. "*Mrmph, mrmph,*" confirmed that my mouth had been sealed with duct tape, and that it was going to hurt if I continued to try to shout. No sense thinking about the back of my head or the sticky, coppery-smelling puddle underneath it. Nodding off again wasn't going to do me much good, either, when whoever had whacked me on the noggin came back to do a better job of it.

I was probably concussed, and I was definitely trussed. Lying on a cellar floor, tied by the wrists to the fanciest leg of my uncle's workbench, I was sorely in need of an exit plan.

OK then. One step at a time.

Step One: Find something to loosen the knots. Maybe Uncle Charlie had left some helpful tool under his workbench? No. Uncle Charlie clearly was not the sort to misplace his tools. Aunt Amy, however, was. Yep. Under her nearby craft table was a moldy ball of yarn, an antiquated darning egg, yellowing needlepoint canvases, assorted knitting needles, and two dead mice.

Wait. Knitting needles.

When we were quite young, Uncle Charlie took it upon himself to teach his daughters and the

Marshall girls how to sail. He spent many hours patiently explaining the basics of navigation, providing us with hands-on experience on the boats, and skippering with us in the Junior Pram races at the Nantucket Yacht Club. He also taught us knots — bowlines, anchor bends, clove hitches — and he taught us how to undo them. Quickly. You never knew when you would need an emergency release of some line to prevent capsizing or crashing.

You also never knew when you might find yourself trussed like a Christmas goose in a cellar.

Step Two: Get one of the knitting needles. Having no hands available for the job, I realized Step Two would have to be done with some fancy footwork instead. Which could then lead to a Step Three: untie the knots, and the great escape would be underway.

Historically, there have been many great real-life escapes by inventive, determined prisoners, and I was pointlessly reminding myself of the report Rory Cheff, eighth grade smart aleck, gave a few weeks ago on the very same topic.

"In 1755, Giacomo Casanova was sentenced to serve five years in prison for repeated adultery," began Rory to an already sniggering class. "Is there anyone who doesn't know what adultery means?" he asked all innocent-eyed, but unquestionably up to no good. Rory was playing the adolescent class well, many of whom were in on the gig.

As if she were merely seeking to enrich her stunted vocabulary, Sonia inquired with phony curiosity. "*I* don't know what adultery means, Rory. *Would* you mind explaining it?"

Hoping to head off Rory's uncensored and sure to titillate definition, I interrupted with a dry, Webster-like version, focusing more on betrayal of marriage vows than sex. Quick-thinking Rory delivered his punch lines anyway using "sex addict" at least three times, "sexaholic" twice, and airily rhyming "Venetian stronghold for an unrepentant cuckold" to describe the Leads prison from which Casanova escaped. The middle school crowd loved it.

Although Rory next gave an uneventful report on Henry Brown, a runaway slave who had his friends nail him up in a box and ship him to the Pennsylvania Anti-Slavery Society, his account of Buffalo Bill Cody's daring escape from a horde of wild Indians incited hooting applause from his already well-primed audience.

ACK ATTACK

Apparently, Buffalo Bill's Sioux captors were nearly starving and running out of meat. Convincing them that he knew of a nearby cattle herd they could scavenge, Cody mounted a long-toothed, borrowed mule and rode off at the head of the eager raiding party. Once the would-be cattle thieves were away from camp, Cody kicked his mount into a desperate canter. For the entire six-mile chase, Buffalo Bill evaded arrows, spears, and recapture, eventually escaping his pursuers by hiding out in a saloon in Ft. Larned, Kansas.

"*Soooooo*," mocked Rory, "the famous Buffalo Bill, that heroic American icon Wild Bill Cody, made an *ass*tonishing *ass*cape on the back of an ass." Adolescent potty talk thrives on puns, innuendos, and jokes, usually at some adult's expense. Rory is a master.

My own great escape would have to be far more run-of-the-mill. To affect it, I would need to execute my first decidedly lackluster feat: take off my shoes. Barefooted, I might stand a chance at getting a grip on one of the forgotten knitting needles. Shoes levered off and zeroed in on the largest needle, I heel-rolled it out into the open, applied just-so pressure to the head of it, and managed to raise the pointy end of it up a precarious inch or two.

Now, steady...steady...and, snatch- grab it as fast as lightning.

Lightning-fast has never been a calibration on my speedometer. I have many degrees of slow-but-steady. None for lightning-fast. Nonetheless, ten or twenty tries later, I had it. Not with anything resembling a lightning speed snatch, however. More like a series of repeated, creaky, slow-motion maneuvers: rolling the ball of yarn out from under the workbench; toe nudging the pointy end of the knitting needle up on the side of it; steadying the yarn with the left foot; gripping the knitting needle with the right.

Grab it, squeeze it, and for crying out loud, don't let go.

Feeling somewhat like an over-ambitious yogi, I then jacked my feet up toward my hands, held the needle with the best death grip I could muster, and jimmied it into the first loop I could find. Once that knot was wiggled loose, I jabbed for the next one. Jab, wiggle, poke, gouge. Unsteady and trembling, knot by knot, I'd worked them loose.

Freed of the workbench, I set about Step Four: sit up, stand up, and cook up a Step Five. Overly eager to implement the as yet unformulated Step Five, I sat up quickly and fell over even quicker. Just like the tricycle guy in the old seventies show *Laugh-In* — without a twitch, flinch, or a flail. *Thunk.*

With a bit more caution, I tried it again. Sat up, stayed up, *and* stood up. Convinced that standing up was as far as my great escape would go for the time being, I contentedly rested my head on the oaken boards of the workbench, ready to enjoy a well-earned nap. I smelled traces of the lemon oil Uncle Charlie had massaged regularly into the oak top. Involuntary memories of the many happy hours I had spent down here with my uncle threatened to dull the indispensable edge of my anger.

Stop it, Margaret Marshall! No room for nostalgia, naps, or self-pity in these escape plans. Well, maybe a smattering of self-pity was allowed. After all, why was no one missing me? I heard no hue and cry. No alarms sounding. No thundering footsteps madly combing every inch of the grounds to find me. I didn't expect bloodhounds, but...well, *something*.

If I continued thinking along those lines, I would dissolve.

"Bootstraps!" Aunt Amy would have instructed. "Pull yourself up by the bootstraps. No lollygagging and whimpering."

Mom weighed in next with some advice of her own. "Just do the next best thing."

The next best thing was to cut the duct tape binding my wrists together. I could see Uncle Charlie's favorite filleting knife carefully outlined by its white perimeter, hanging up in its place on the wall—a good fifteen inches above the top of the workbench. To reach it, I would have to get on top of the workbench—quite the task for a scuffed up senior citizen with firmly bound wrists.

Not sure if my derring-do had enough do left in it, I rested my upper body weight on my elbows, gasped in a couple breaths, and swung my legs upward. Although I gave myself credit for a laudably valiant attempt, truth be told, my derring-do was all done in. Completely tuckered out. I would just have to fashion some sort of ladder and prosaically inchworm my way up onto the top of the workbench. So much for swashbuckling.

When I was a girl, it seemed as if most summer days were sunny and spent outside, usually at the beach.

However, even in my childhood's Nantucket, it sometimes rained. Most rainy days were spent at my aunt's house in the playroom with my cousins, enjoying the dolls, dresser-size dollhouse, and the miniature furniture that Uncle Charlie had made for us. We spent hours and hours role-playing domestic life, sewing doll clothes out of fabric scraps, and making wallpaper for the tiny rooms with paint-by-numbers oil painting kits.

Now, each summer Josh organizes his cousins to help him get the dollhouse up from the cellar to the playroom. The successive generations still play exactly as we did: imagining, creating, and passing their own rainy days. In the winter, the dollhouse returns to the cellar for repairs and sits just to the right of the workbench — exactly where it sat now, and just as heavy and solid as I remembered it. It was just the right height for my "ladder," *if* I could figure out how to move it closer to the workbench.

A right-shouldered push didn't work; neither did a left-shouldered one. Pushing with my back wasn't much better. The dollhouse just wasn't budging.

When Elvis Presley made his first television appearance on *The Ed Sullivan Show* in 1956, we sat down as a family to watch. One look at the slicked-back ducktail and the gyrating pelvis, and my dad snapped the TV right off. "You girls will not watch that greaser, that...*hood*!" Greaser sounded like something one would scrape off the bottom of a shoe. Hood sounded worse.

Naturally, we spent a lot of time at friends' houses and never missed a single one of Elvis's televised performances. We listened to his music every chance we got and bought every single one of his 45 RPM records. We watched Elvis, we adored Elvis, and we learned how to dance just like he did. Our pelvic thrusts and hip-waggles were the envy of the neighborhood.

Hip bumps and pelvic thrusts would be just the thing to move a substantial dollhouse. I'd worry about bruises and splintered hip bones tomorrow.

Bump, grind. Thrust, shove. Half an inch, an inch...a quarter of an inch...another half an inch. Mighty slow progress, but it worked.

Getting on top of the dollhouse was next. Grunt, grunt, heave-ho. One more heaving ho, and I was kneeling on the dollhouse. More of the same got me from the top of the dollhouse to the top of the workbench—looking right at Aunt Amy.

"Who's there? What's going on down there?" she demanded, peering down at me through the window.

"Mrmph! Mrmph!"

"Maggie? What in the world...?"

More *murmph*-ing wasn't going to do me much good.

"Tied up! Oh, my dear! You're tied up. Bound and gagged!"

And she vanished. Just left.

Surely she was going for help? Not from Frick or Frack, I hoped. Minutes that seemed like hours passed before I heard a shrill, "*Pssst! Pssst!*"

Aunt Amy had snuck into the cellar, probably through the old coal chute by the looks of her— black soot from head to toe. "Get down. Get down, right now," she ordered. "I've got a knife."

Generally, when Aunt Amy orders me around, I openly defy her or passively resist. Not this time. Only too happy to have a domineering, soot-covered, slightly loopy rescuer bossing me around,

I did my best to comply and got shakily down much the same way I had gotten up.

"Hold still, damn it!" she hissed. My quavering earned me a few knife nicks, but the ropes were cut faster than I would have expected for two frenetic bumblers. My desperate *mrmph, mrmph*-ing led Aunt Amy to my duct-taped mouth. She loosened a corner and began to peel — way too slowly, way too painfully. More desperate *mrmph*-ing, this time accompanied by No! No! head shaking. As hoped, Aunt Amy gave up the peeling.

"*Shhhh!*" she barked unnecessarily. "Up the coal chute. Let's go. Hurry."

Although I wasn't physically in any kind of hurry-up condition, I managed to follow Aunt Amy up the chute using a fairly effective elbow crawl. *She* crawled up as if she had just graduated from boot camp. Vigorous, efficient, and energetic, my aunt was at the top of the chute in no time, peeking through the trapdoor to see if the way was clear for our escape.

It wasn't. She slowly lowered the trapdoor and signaled for me to freeze. We waited, and then she took a second peek and made the A-OK sign.

"Well, come *on!*" she commanded. "Oh, for heaven's sake. Here, take my hand." Apparently, three more feet of chute crawling was more than I could manage on my own.

Out in the open air, wheezing and panting, we crouched behind her just-leafing Lacecap hydrangeas. Because my aunt's prized bushes had (of course) been properly pruned last fall, there was scant cover for us. If we hoped to be screened at all from passersby, we'd have to squat down impossibly low. Not sure if I wanted anything to do with a prolonged deep knee bend, I signed that I thought lying down instead might be a nice option. A refreshing nap for a couple of days would be just the thing.

Not Aunt Amy. "Hey! You three! Put 'em up!"

Jiminy Christmas. She had her gun.

Weapon drawn, she charged John Wayne-style across the side lawn, shouting at the three figures kneeling on Senator Marques's concrete pad: Boston, Frick, and Frack. Protectively flanked by Frick and Frack, Boston was hunkered down by the air conditioning unit intently adjusting something inside of it. Immediately, both Frick and Frack drew out their weapons. They looked ready — even eager — to use them.

"Help! Help! Someone help me!"

The cry for help should have been coming from me or from my aunt. It wasn't. It was coming from Ernie Whitehead with Sundance, followed by Bonnie, Clyde, and Butch, nipping at his heels. Ernie was running faster than I would have thought possible for an old gimper — arms pumping, feet racing, camera bouncing wildly on the strap around his neck.

"Call them off, call them off!" he shouted, spotting my aunt. Oblivious to the fact that he was smack dab in the middle of an armed standoff, Ernie raced toward Aunt Amy, renewing his pleas for help.

"Sic 'em!" she hollered.

Thinking that this was a heck of a time to get even with Ernie, I stood up, hoping to call off the dogs. No need. Aunt Amy wasn't pointing at Ernie; she was pointing at Frick and Frack. The dogs, obedient for possibly the first time in their lives, whirled around to find the newly designated targets. With Sundance in the lead, they snarled, dashed, and leaped just as Cousin Elizabeth, David, Josh, and Chloe rushed around the corner.

Dogs baying, people shouting — it was enough of a ruckus to scare up a whole kit and caboodle of Secret Service agents, local cops, and the rest of my picnicking family.

Click. Click. Click.

Ernie Whitehead. Soot-faced, gun-toting Aunt Amy had been captured on film.

Click. Click. Frenzied dogs on the attack, also on film.

Click. Me. Soot-faced and duct-taped.

The next Neighborhood Association meeting was going to be a blood bath.

CHAPTER 17—The Hospital

"You're coming with me to the hospital. No arguments, young lady," David laughed.

No arguments indeed. My mouth was taped shut—a perfect opportunity for him to deliver one of his what-the-hell-were-you-thinking lectures without any interruptions.

I was grateful for his firm grip on my elbow, but not for the direction we were going: toward his car and away from all the commotion. Craning my woozy head back around, I could see that Boston was in cuffs, Frick and Frack were spread-eagled on the ground, and Ernie was getting the licking of his life—from Butch and Bonnie. I could hear official-type voices loudly barking orders. Cousin Elizabeth was squealing, the triplets were bawling, and Jackie was hollering up a blue streak, calling Boston every name in the book.

ACK ATTACK

Trying to jerk free of David's persuasive grip was a mistake. As my peripheral vision blurred, colors turned that wavy, yellow-green again. My ears buzzed, and my knees folded out from under me.

I woke up to ole Doc McGruder stretching my left lid open, searing its eyeball with a little white light. "Well, well, Maggie," he drawled. "It was a pleasure bringing you into this world. Wouldn't have been one to see you out of it."

"Not ready to go just yet, Doc," I replied.

Replied?

Ahhhh, the tape had been removed—none too gently, judging by my blistering lips.

"Is David still here?" I asked. "I'm ready to go home now."

David was still there, but I wasn't going home.

He didn't even bother to argue with me. "I'll go see about getting her admittance forms completed. Brenda said she's got a bed ready for her in the ICU. Jackie's coming in as soon as the police are finished with her."

274

"Maggie'll be ready for ICU observation as soon as I get her stitched up."

A good night's sleep can do wonders. I awakened in the ICU to David's snoring and Jackie's cussing. David was keeping watch (in a fashion) from an uncomfortable-looking bedside chair. Jackie was pacing and talking on her cell phone, wrapping up a few Boston-related loose ends with the cops. If the police had had any doubts about the disreputable depths of Boston's character, they certainly didn't now.

As rumored, Boston wasn't his name. He was Tyrone Jackson, father of three and wanted in Mississippi for armed robbery. Sensing I was awake, Jackie ended the call and holstered her phone.

Her surprisingly gentle, "Hey, sis," rallied David, and the two of them fiddled and fussed with dripping bags and soggy dressings. Neither expressed any interest in humoring me with a ride home. I resigned myself to their ministrations, kept my bruised mouth shut, and dozed on the gurney as they wheeled me from the ICU to my room. I was sleeping soundly before they had finished tucking me in.

"Me. *I'm* the one who found her. Not a one of you even knew she was missing." Aunt Amy was bragging when I came to.

"The 'she' is awake. No more talking about me."

Although the yellow and green colors were gone, my head was still rather echoey, and the rest of me felt like it had been hit by the proverbial truck. Probably looked like it, too, judging from the size of the bandage on my head, the cuts on my hands, and the bruises on my wrists. Although I wondered vaguely about hip splinters and pulled muscles, I figured that whatever Doc MacGruder had dripping from the IV would keep worry and pain at a minimum.

"Well, I'll be switched." Chloe's inimitable expression of surprise. "You're awake!"

"Why aren't you on the plane? Chelsea's baby?" I asked as she and Brett came in with an armload of flowers. Shad was right behind them with a box of saltines, a six-pack of ginger ale, and what smelled like a bag of breakfast burritos.

"Not a chance we'd be leaving this island until Chloe was sure you were all right," answered Brett.

"Sheesh, Ma. You coulda been killed!"

Surrounded by my family, snug in a hospital bed, "killed" didn't seem very likely. In fact, the whole incident was more like one of those vague recollections that may or may not have happened at all. Although I knew that I was probably not firing on all cylinders, I insisted on hearing exactly what *had* happened: who had hit me on the head, who had locked me in the cellar, and what Boston was doing with Frick and Frack?

Everyone, as usual, started talking at once.

Despite the ever increasing volume of the cross talk, my muzzy-headed thinking, and the constant flow of interruptions, I got the gist of what had happened back at Aunt Amy's — or at least as much as they knew.

As I understood it, Aunt Amy and I had caught Boston in the act of tinkering with the air conditioning unit at Senator Marques's. Frick and Frack had been standing on guard to make sure that Boston's tinkering went unnoticed. My earlier stumbling upon Boston's tool belt had them all on full alert.

ACK ATTACK

"But Aunt Amy, how did you know where to find me?"

"Detective work. I easily deduced —"

"Detective work, my arseket," interrupted Jackie. "Didn't you wander off to check on your tea roses? I don't seem to recall that it had anything to do with Maggie."

No one was taking the wind out of her sails. "Ruse. Purely a ruse."

Brett snorted. Shad rolled her eyes.

All were in agreement about one thing, however: it was probably Boston who had clobbered and tethered me. "Bet he was just tickled to have *that* opportunity," Jackie said.

"In fact, I don't know why he didn't just finish you off," agreed Chloe.

"Outfoxed him. Foiled his plan." Not to be sidetracked, Aunt Amy was off and running, colorfully describing the part she had played in the rescue. "Shimmied down the coal chute, cut Maggie free, and, lickety split, pulled her out." She actually puffed out her chest.

278

Well into the spirit of the self-congratulatory heroics, David gave my aunt a parody of a full military honors salute. Joining in the leg pulling, Chloe gave a poor imitation of Kate Smith singing the first few lines of "The Star-Spangled Banner."

"All right, already. Enough. Please, Chloe, no more singing. What *was* going on at the senator's?" I persisted.

"Stonewalled. Those agents won't tell us a thing," huffed Aunt Amy. "Questions. That's all we get. Questions and no answers. Why, I have a mind—"

"Burrito, Mrs. Delano?" asked David, successfully cutting short her harangue.

Not quite up to a burrito but definitely ready for something, I cranked up the back of the bed and surveyed the miscellanea on top of my roll-around table: Kleenex; one of those U-shaped, plastic, throw-up basins; and a pitcher of iced water. There was also a breakfast tray bearing lumpy porridge, unbuttered toast, and lukewarm beef broth.

"Here, Ma, try this." Ah, Shad, with crackers and ginger ale.

"Oh, no. What day is it? Is it Tuesday?" I asked a bit frantically.

"Tuesday, and don't worry, your classes are covered—I called the school this morning. The office was going to line up Mrs. Sheller to cover your classes for at least the rest of the week," David informed me.

"Poor kids," I commiserated. "Thanks, David."

"You owe me. Again," he replied. "This dramatic hair raiser of yours won't get you out of our date," he added rather cagily. "Saturday night. That gives you four days to recover."

Arched eyebrows all around the room, but no one said a word. Dead silence, a rare commodity in my family.

Mike Gaspee's brisk entrance broke the high voltage silence. His bedraggled uniform and red-rimmed eyes indicated that he probably had not gotten any sleep the previous night. His stifled yawn and wearily offered "Morning," confirmed that he was just about at the end of his tether. His obvious exhaustion didn't stop anyone from peppering him with questions.

"Whoa. Whoa," he responded, half backing out of the room. "I just stopped by to see if Maggie was all right. I'll tell you what I can, but the Secret Service has taken over the entire investigation." What Mike could tell us was a whole lot more than what we had surmised. However, it was hardly a complete picture. There were still many loose ends and even more dead ones.

Boston/Tyrone was indeed connected to Frick, Frack, the three Scowlies, and Senator Marques, who was in fact hosting a secret meeting of world leaders. Although I am certain that Jackie's rapid-fire questioning and Aunt Amy's incessant tangents had already wheedled out more information than Mike was supposed to give us, we continued to fire questions until he wisely called it to a halt.

"Gotta go," explained Mike. "I'm expected back at the station in two hours, and if I don't get some sleep—"

"Go. Rest. And here, take a burrito with you. Thanks for all your help," soothed Chloe, seeing him out the door.

"Well, damn it," I grumped. "So what *did* happen?"

ACK ATTACK

Brett seemed to have the clearest picture and the most commanding voice. He slowly recapped Mike's somewhat haphazard explanation to his increasingly astonished audience. The meeting at Senator Marques's was, as the newspaper had reported, a high-level conference between some pretty impressive dignitaries. And yes, the secretary of state as well as leaders of Afghanistan, Iraq, and the OPEC cartel had all been there.

The American Aryan Party, thanks to their contacts within our government, had gained advanced knowledge of the meeting and targeted it for a biochemical attack. The treasonous Frick and Frack had given the terrorist cell all the insider information it needed to orchestrate the entire operation.

"Scowlies! What about them? Those Scowlies?" demanded my aunt.

"Was Mom *right*?" asked Shad. "Were those three part of it?"

It seems they were. The Three Scowlies were fanatical white nationalists recently recruited by the Aryans to carry out acts of domestic terrorism that would further the organization's racist, xenophobic agenda. Knowing that Nantucket is the

282

vacation destination for many international movers and shakers, these rogue neo-Nazi isolationists had come to the island earlier in the year. Once here, they had quietly established residency in a basement apartment on Macy Lane, gotten part-time jobs with Aden House Painters, and kept a low profile. They were just waiting for the right situation and the right time.

The summit was the perfect opportunity. Using the detailed information about the meeting supplied by Frick and Frack, they slowly fine-tuned their plan. With frequent trips off island and careful shopping on the internet, they stockpiled the chemicals and equipment they would need to make the deadly sarin gas.

"The bunker out at Tom Nevers was their lab, right?" Jackie asked. "We even have pictures. Maggie, where's your phone?" Not waiting for a response from me, she rifled through the blue plastic hospitality bag provided by the ER. "The pictures are not very clear, but look here; you can see the stuff—well, sort of. Here, look at this one. How about this one?"

Judging by the dubious squints, we had captured only opaque images and shadowy impressions.

Nothing substantive. "Well, the Feds will have gone out there by now. *They'll* get the evidence," Jackie assured us. "What I still don't understand is why Boston was involved."

"Money—what else?" offered Shad. "But what could they possibly be paying him for?"

David picked up where Brett had left off. "Mike indicated that Boston was hired to rig a valve in the condenser unit of Senator Marques's air conditioner. He was also supposed to put plastic bags filled with sarin inside the unit and attach some puncturing apparatus near the bags. Once the bags were in place, he'd set a timer, open the valves, close up the air conditioner, and get out of Dodge."

Brett finished the explanation. "Once the bags were pierced, the sarin would filter through the ducts, probably killing most everyone in the house."

"And you guys with your beach picnic were a serendipitous diversion," added David. "Something to keep the attention of the other Secret Service agents diverted from what they were up to."

"But why did Boston leave Maggie alive?" Jackie wondered aloud.

"He probably had to get the go-ahead from the agents, your Frick and Frack guys," David speculated.

"Or maybe, for whatever else he is, he drew the line at murder," Chloe suggested.

"Saved the day! Caught 'em in the nick of time. Rescued Maggie, then captured the bad guys." There was going to be no living with Aunt Amy for quite a while.

Denouement had been one of last week's eighth grade vocabulary challenges. It was a Stumper: none of the students knew what it meant. Anytime we run into a Stumper, the vocabulary challenge becomes a race through the dictionary. Charlotte, our usual Stumper Champ, had found it first for double points.

Charlotte found that denouement means the final resolution of a plot, a story, or a complex sequence of events. Denouement could not be applied to our puzzle. Pieces were still missing and dots weren't connecting. However, as far as Aunt Amy was concerned, the crisis was over and she was the

ACK ATTACK

center stage heroine. Co-starring in her drama: Butch, Sundance, Bonnie, and Clyde.

"Coldcocked 'em. Knocked 'em right on the ground. The dogs took care of all of 'em...even that Ernie Whitehead."

Braggadocio. Perfect for next week's vocabulary challenge.

"How's the patient this morning?" Doc McGruder walked in, looking as dapper as always, a medical version of Mr. Chips.

As before, David and Jackie discussed my condition with Doc as if I weren't there. Irked at being referred to as "the patient" and discussed in the third person, I swung my legs over the side of the bed and stood up. "I'm going home."

Shad caught me just before I hit the floor. She and Chloe eased me back onto the bed. Doc, David, and Jackie continued talking just as before.

Perhaps I would just take a nap. Maybe when I woke up, they'd all be gone.

Swat! "Maggie. Hey, Maggie." Swat, swat! "Look at this." Another swat.

286

I opened my eyes. Aunt Amy was swatting away at my shoulder with a newspaper. "Me. It's me. Front page."

Yup, there she was on the front page of this morning's *Boston Globe*, covered in soot, hair spiked with grime, grinning maniacally, and pointing her gun. The headline was huge. In bold print, all capital letters, and some enormous, authoritative font: SENIOR SAVES THE DAY. The caption under her picture read, "Nantucket senior Amy-Ann Compton Delano foils neo-Nazi plot."

The article went on to summarize the events, speculate about implications, and describe Aunt Amy as if she were a national hero worthy of sainthood. She read every single word of that article. Out loud. She read the paragraphs that were specifically about her at least twice.

Ad nauseam. Another great vocabulary challenge.

Doc McGruder, who had delivered the newspaper, slipped out sometime during the second reading of the third page. Shad had been reading over Aunt Amy's shoulder. "Here, let me see. There's more on the front page. Look!"

There was a picture of Ernie Whitehead looking rabidly furious, with one eye swollen shut, the other narrowed and mean. The photographer had caught him with his mouth twisting in a vicious snarl and his foot planted in Butch's side. The dogs' role in thwarting "an international terrorist plot" was described in glowing praise. Ernie's role in gumming up the works was described in wonderfully damning detail.

Aunt Amy would have no trouble at the next Neighborhood Association meeting. I might even go along to enjoy the show. The show that I wouldn't enjoy was the family meeting that would surely result after everyone read the follow-up article on page four:

"State Health Department officials call for an investigation into allegations of poisoning at Sherburne Commons, Nantucket's senior community."

No one would need to speculate about who had made the allegations. There she was. Again. No gun in the picture this time, just a poster that read, Sherburne Residents Being Doped.

"Main Street. Main Street, here I come," crowed Aunt Amy.

"Don't count on it." I might have been concussed, but I was clear-headed enough to realize that the family would have to reconsider its strategy to keep Aunt Amy out of her Main Street house and safely tucked away in Sherburne each winter. We were no match for her. Aunt Amy could out-manipulate Machiavelli.

"Come on, you old troublemaker. I'm taking you home." Jackie, clearly done-in, made one last check of the various machines on the wall behind my bed and then boosted Aunt Amy out of her chair.

Brett was suddenly all a-bustle. "We're heading out, too. We're on standby for the twelve thirty flight. Gotta pack, close down the house."

A hug from Chloe accompanied her admonishment. "Could you just stay out of trouble for the next week or so 'til we get back?"

Shad was getting up, too. "I'm going home to update the Sibs and grab a nap myself. I'll be back later with a nightgown, underwear, and your toothbrush. You want anything else?"

"Socks. And chocolate."

I caught her cutting her eyes at David. The two of them were in cahoots, and judging by the barely perceptible shake of David's head, I wasn't getting any chocolate.

When they all left, I would hightail it to the gift shop and get my own dang chocolate.

He must have read my mind. "Better bring her some. She'll just sneak off and get some out of the vending machines."

As they all trickled out, I settled in for a much-needed nap.

I opened one eye. David was still there.

"You can go. I'll behave."

He settled himself as best he could in the uncomfortable vinyl chair. "I'm not going anywhere. You're stuck with me."

Mmmmmmmm.

ABOUT THE AUTHOR

Dennie lives, teaches, gardens, and writes on Nantucket.

Made in the USA
Charleston, SC
22 March 2012